John Newton Stearns

Merry's Rhymes and Puzzles

John Newton Stearns

Merry's Rhymes and Puzzles

ISBN/EAN: 9783337273262

Printed in Europe, USA, Canada, Australia, Japan

Cover: Foto ©Andreas Hilbeck / pixelio.de

More available books at **www.hansebooks.com**

MERRY'S

BOOK OF PUZZLES.

EDITED BY ROBERT MERRY.

NEW YORK:
THOMAS O'KANE, PUBLISHER,
130 NASSAU STREET.

PREFACE.

THE innumerable readers of MERRY'S MUSEUM will here meet with many familiar faces, lighted up by pleasant smiles, and hear the same old jovial laughter that greeted them in the olden time.

Our motto is that of our noble State—"EXCELSIOR!" Our readers will see that we have not buried the talents of our contributors in napkins—but seek to bring them out into the bright day: For Genius —like the lamp of Aladdin—needs constant polishing to bring out its lustre and full effect.

Our object has been to instruct by smiles—not frowns; to cheer the dear hearts of the young girlhood and boyhood; to strew flowers among the necessary thorns of existence. In a word, we try in these pages to make the sad happy—the happy still happier.

Hence, pure fun will be found as beautiful in these pages, as honey amid the flowers of Hybla

ROBERT MERRY.

ROBERT MERRY to his friends
A kindly greeting sends,
With a general assortment of questions,
Conundrums, Charades,
Puzzles, Riddles of all shades,
And Rebuses, as aids
To intellectual and social digestion.

If the young Merry host
Acquaintance should boast,
Or kindred, or authorship pat,
With some of our jokes,
We confess—('tis no hoax)—
To amuse other folks,
We have *riddled* the Museum "Chat."

Now we beg you will show,
If you happen to know,
Why the Editor, painstaking soul?
Is like the cold storm
Which, in climates bright and warm,
Where gallinippers swarm,
Come shivering down from the pole?

1.

2.

3. Who prolongs his work to as great a length as pos-sible, and still completes it in time?

4. Why are young ladies like arrows?

5. Why is a philanthropist like an old horse?

6. How can five persons divide five eggs, so that each man shall receive one, and still one remain in the dish?

7. How many soft-boiled eggs could the giant Goliah eat upon an empty stomach?

8. What fishes have their eyes nearest together?

9. Two fathers have each a square of land. One father divides his so as to reserve to himself one-fourth in the form of a square; thus—

The other father divides his so as to reserve to himself one-fourth in the form of a triangle; thus—

They each have four sons, and each divides the remainder among his sons in such a way that each son will share equally with his brother, and in similar shape. How were the two farms divided?

10.

11.

12. What is that which is often brought to table, often cut, but never eaten?

13. My first is four-sixths of a step that is long,
    My second is a person of state;
  My whole is a thing that is known to be wrong,
    And is a strong symptom of hate.

14. Why are your nose and chin always at variance?

15.   Without my first you can not stand,
    My second beauteous fair command;
    Together I attend your will,
    And am your humble servant still.

16. Why ought a fisherman to be very wealthy?

17. Why is a man in debt like a misty morning?

18. Who was the first that bore arms?

19. There is a word of seven letters; the first two refers to man, the first three refers to woman, the first four signifies a great man, the seven a great woman.

20. I am a word of five letters. Take away my first and I am the name of what adorns the estate of many of the nobility of England. Take away my first and second, and I am the name of a place where all the world was once congregated. Take away my last, and I am the name of a beautiful mineral. Take away my two last, and I am the name of a fashionable place of resort. I am small in stature, but capable of doing a great deal of mischief, as I once did in London in the year 1666.

21. Spell eye-water four letters.

22. Why is swearing like an old coat?

23. Why is a thump like a hat?

24. Why is an inn like a burial-ground?

25.

26.

27. If a fender cost six dollars, what will a ton of coal come to?

28. What word is that to which if you add a syllable, it will make it shorter?

29. My first is a very uncomfortable state,
   In cold weather it mostly abounds.
   My second's an instrument formed of hard steel,
   That will cause the stout foe to stagger and reel,
   And when used, is a symptom of hate.
   My whole is an author of greatest renown,
   Whose fame to the last day of time will go down.

30. What is the longest and yet the shortest thing in the world; the swiftest and yet the slowest; the most divisible and the most extended; the least valued and the most regretted; without which nothing can be done; which devours every thing, however small, and yet gives life and spirits to every object, however great?

31.   My first is found in every house,
      From wintry winds it guards.
   My second is the highest found—
      In every pack of cards.
   My whole, a Scottish chief, is praised
      By ballad, bard, and story,
   Who for his country gave his life,
      And, dying, fell with glory.

32. Why are handsome women like bread?

33. Why is an avaricious man like one with a short memory?

34. What river in Bavaria answers the question, Who is there?

35. Why is a man with wooden legs like one who has an even bargain?

36.

37.

38. Why is a parish bell like a good story?

39. What belongs to yourself, yet is used by others more than yourself?

40. In camps about the centre I appear;
 In smiling meadows seen throughout the year;
 The silent angler views me in the streams,
 And all must trace me in their morning dreams,
 First in the mob conspicuous I stand,
 Proud of the lead, and ever in command.

41. The head of a whale is six feet long; his tail is as long as his head and half his body, and his body is half of his whole length. How long is the whale?

42. A hundred stones are placed, in a straight line, a yard distant from each other. How many yards must a person walk, who undertakes to pick them up, and place them in a basket stationed one yard from the first stone?

43. My first is a part of the day,
  My last a conductor of light,
  My whole to take measure of time,
   Is useful by day and by night.

44. I am a word of three syllables, each of which is a word; my first is an article in common use; my second, an animal of uncommon intelligence; my third, though not an animal, is used in carrying burdens. My whole is a useful art.

45. There was a man who was *not* born,
  His father was *not* born before him,
  He did *not* live, he did *not* die,
  And his epitaph is *not* o'er him.

46. Why is a nail, fast in the wall, like an old man?

47. Why does a miller wear a white hat?

48.

49.

50. My first is a letter commanding to wed,
   Or to lift your sole till it reaches your head;
   Nothing worth as a whole, it is plain to all men
   That divided in halves, it is equal to ten;

My second, though nothing, compared to the other,
Is worth more as a partner than its double-faced brother;
It moans and it sighs, and when joined to my first,
Pronounces the doom of the sinner accursed.

My third, you will find his whole value depends
On the worth and position of neighbors and friends,
And, when both the other two following fair,
Changes doom to desire, and a curse to a prayer.

My fourth, though it formeth no part of a hundred,
Shows where it can justly and evenly be sundered;
'Tis found in the elements everywhere present,
'Tis found in all seasons, unpleasant or pleasant,
'Tis the chief of all lands, and yet can not wait
On continent, hemisphere, empire, or state.
Though ne'er in Great Britain suspected to lower,
'Tis the heart of each quarter of that mighty power;
It always belonged to the animal race,
In the mineral kingdom they gave it a place,
And, being impartial, they could not deny,
The vegetable order its virtue to try;
And yet, since creation, it never was known
In beast, bird, or fish, root, branch, stem, or stone.

My whole you'll find growing in pasture and barns,
Or grown in coats, carpets, warm blankets, and yarns,
In England, in Saxony, France, and old Wales,
And in sundry more places it always prevails.
Of quadrupedal origin—still it is known
In bipedal families oft to be shown;   [tions
But the strangest of all its strange forms and condi-
Is seen in the covering of sage politicians.

51.

52.

53. What is that which is invisible, but never out of sight?

54. When is a boat like a knife?

55. What part of London is in France?

56. How many black beans will make five white ones?

57. Why is a dandy like a haunch of venison?

58. What kin is that child to its father who is not its father's own son?

59. Why is a rose-bud like a promissory note?

60. What biblical name is there which expresses a father calling his son by name, and his son replying?

61. Why is an orange not like a church bell?

62. Why is the largest city in Ireland likely to be the largest city in the world?

63. Three-fourths of a cross, and a circle complete,
    An upright where two semicircles meet,
    A rectangle triangle standing on feet,
    Two semicircles, and a circle complete.

64. What smells most in a drug shop?

65. Why should doctors attend to window-sashes?

66. G. a. $\frac{P}{A}$.

67. What is that which every one can divide, but no one can see where it has been divided?

68. Spell hard water with three letters.

69. What letters of the alphabet come too late for supper?

70.

71.

72. Pronounced as one letter, and written with three,
Two letters there are, and two only in me ;
I'm double, I'm single, I'm black, blue, and gray,
I am read from both ends, and the same either way,
I am restless and wandering, steady and fixed,
And you know not one hour what I may be the next.
I melt, and I kindle—beseech, and defy,
I am watery and moist, I am fiery and dry.
I am scornful and scowling, compassionate, meek ;
I am light, I am dark, I am strong, I am weak.
I'm piercing and clean, I am heavy and dull ;
Expressive and languid, contracted and full.
I'm a globe and a mirror, a window, a door,
An index, an organ, and fifty things more.
I belong to all animals under the sun,
And to those who were long understood to have
    none.
My language is plain, though it can not be heard,
And I speak without even pronouncing a word.
Some call me a diamond—some say I am jet ;
Others talk of my water, or how I am set.
I'm a borough in England, in Scotland a stream,
And an isle of the sea in the Irishman's dream.
The earth without me would no loveliness wear,
And sun, moon, and stars at my wish disappear.
Yet so frail is my tenure, so brittle my joy,
That a speck gives me pain, and a drop can destroy.

73. What vessel is that which is always asking leave
to move ?

74. Translate the following into Latin—
        42, 8 rocks, e e e e e e e e e e, 46. 2. 14. 5. 0.

75. How is it that you can work with an awl, but not
with a forceps ; while I can work with a forceps, and not
with an awl ?

76.

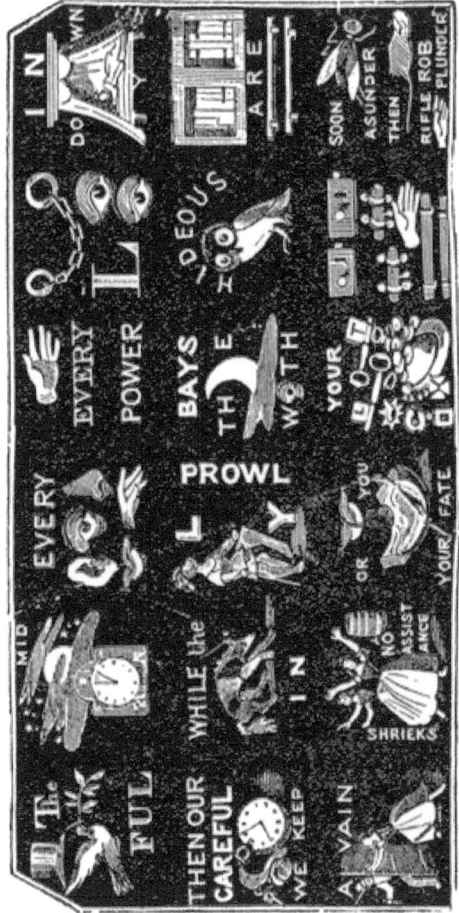

77. *Add*, was the word the master gave to Dick,
Dick scratched his head, and looking rather thick,
Replied, " *Hereafter it would make it stick.*"
" Dick," cried the master, " rudeness is a sin ;
Behold the stocks, I'll surely put you *in.*"
" That," answered Dick, " won't alter it a feather,
Hereafter it would make it hold together."
" Dick," said the man, " if you insult me so,
Your shoulders and my rod I'll put in *Co.*"
" 'Tis all the same," said Dick, "my worthy master,
Hereafter it would make it stick the faster."

78. Why is France like a skeleton ?

79. Why is a woodman like a stage actor ?

80. Why is the hour of noon on the dial-plate like a pair of spectacles ?

81. Why is the best baker most in want of bread ?

82. Whether old Homer tippled wine or beer,
Julep or cider, history is not clear ;
But plain it is—the bard, though wont to roam,
But for one liquid, never had left home.

83. Why is a coward like a mouse-trap ?

84. Why is green grass like a mouse ?

85. What two reasons why whispering in company is not proper ?

86. My first is found on the ocean wave,
In the spring, the pit, and the mine ;
My second below earth's surface you have,
Where seldom the sun can shine.
My whole your dinner-table must grace,
And seldom fails to obtain a place.

87. Why is a gooseberry pie like counterfeit money ?

88.

89. Why does a fisherman blow his horn?

90. Why is there no danger of starving in a desert?

91.
    Take half of the needle
      By which sailors steer
    Their ship through the water,
      Be it cloudy or clear;
    Do not really break it—
      This of all things were worst—
    But in your mind take it,
      And this makes my first.
    At thanksgiving or Christmas,
      My second you see;
    With care well compounded,
      From grain, shrub, and tree.
    My whole like some people
      Who make great pretense,
    Of words have a plenty,
      But no great stock of sense.

92. How is it that Methuselah was the oldest man, when he died before his father?

93. My first is a negative greatly in use,
By which people begin when they mean to refuse;
My second is Fashion, or so called in France,
But, like other whims, is the servant of chance.
An article always in use is my whole,
With texture and form under fashion's control;
But, alas! not a thing can it see which goes by,
Although many have four sights, and all have one
    eye.

94. What is that which, supposing its greatest breadth to be four inches, length nine inches, and depth three inches, contains a solid foot?

95.

96.   My tongue is long, my breath is strong,
          And yet I breed no strife;
       My voice you hear both far and near,
          And yet I have no life.

97. A waterman rows a given distance, *a*, and back
again in *b* hours, and finds that he can row *c* miles with
the current, for *d* miles against it.   Required, the time of
rowing down, the time of rowing up, the rate of current,
and the rate of rowing.

98. As I was beating on the far east grounds,
       Up starts a hare before my two greyhounds;
       The dogs, being light of foot, did fairly run,
       To her fifteen rods, just twenty-one;
       And the distance that she started up before,
       Was six-and-ninety rods, just and no more;
       Now, I would have you Merry boys declare
       How far they ran, before they caught the hare.

99. Is it possible to put twelve pieces of money in six
rows, and have four in a row?

100. A gentleman sent a servant with a present of nine
ducks, with this direction—
       "To Alderman Gobble, with ix. ducks."
The servant took out three, and contrived it so that the
direction corresponded with the number of the ducks.   He
neither erased nor altered a letter.   How did he do it?

101.   Four letters form me quite complete,
          As all who breathe do show;
        Reversed, you'll find I am the seat
          Of infamy and woe.
        Transposed, you'll see I'm base and mean,
          Again of Jewish race;
        Transposed once more, I oft am seen
          To hide a lovely face.

102.

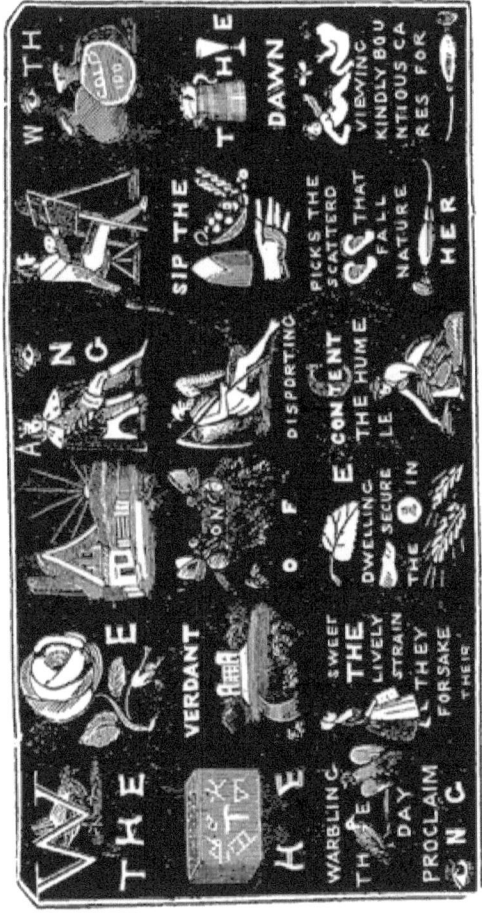

103. My first is the name to an article given
For ladies and dandies to put on their linen ;
It comes from the forest, I've heard people say,
And is made from the skin of an animal gay.
My second is a fruit that comes from the South,
The juice of it is sour, and 'twill pucker your
    mouth ;
'Tis found in candy shops all over the town,
And, stranger to say, it is almost round.
My whole is an article that is often seen
In the gardens and fields almost covered with green;
It is very sweet, and also pleasant to eat,
And in hot summer days affords a rich treat.

104. My first is half of what implies good-humor ; my
second makes sense of my first ; my third sounds like the
cry of a kitten ; my fourth is a consonant and vowel combined ; my fifth, with the addition of the initial of my
third, would imply silence ; and my whole is what many
boys and girls prize highly.

105. I am composed of twelve letters.
My 2, 8, 9, is a substance dug out of the earth.
    " 6, 11, 12, 8, is a numeral.
    " 4, 2, 3, is an ancient instrument of war.
    " 12, 8, 1, is a vessel used in former times.
    " 5, is a vowel.
    " 4, 7, 1, 9, is a hard substance.
    " 10, 9, is a pronoun.
My whole is now before you.

106. My first is appropriate, my second 'tis nine to one
if you guess it. My whole elevates the sole above the
earth.

107. Why is a conundrum like a monkey ?

108. What do we all do when we first get into bed ?

109.

110.

111. There is one word in the English language which is universally considered a preventive of harm; change a certain letter in it, and you make it an act of cruelty.

112. My first may be fashioned of iron or wood,
　　　And at window or door for safety is placed;
　　In village or town it does more harm than good,
　　　Leading people their health, time, and money
　　　　to waste.
　My second's a lady, bewitching and fair,
　　　And for love of her people will labor and strive;
　Will rise before dawn, and be wearied with care,
　　　And pursue her with ardor as long as they live.
　My whole is what ladies admire and approve,
　　　The shopkeeper's boast—the purchaser's prize;
　'Tis a ninepenny chintz—'tis a one-shilling glove—
　　　It is something which makes people open their
　　　　eyes.

113. At what distance must a body have fallen to ac-quire the velocity of 1,600 feet per second?

114. Of what trade is the sun in May?

115. Why is a small horse like a young musk-melon?

116　My first must grace a legal deed,
　　　With its companion, firm and red;
　　Its help in marriage, too, they need,
　　　Before the blessing can be said.
　My second half a hundred is,
　　　If in the shortest way you spell;
　You soon must guess me after this,
　　　I may as well the secret tell.
　My whole, by his celestial strains
　　　Bears the rapt soul to worlds above;
　The Great Creator's power proclaims,
　　　And tells of the Redeemer's love.

117.

118.

119. My first is a boy's nickname; my second is meant for defense; my third is a preposition; my fourth is one of the articles; my fifth is one of the United States. My whole is a large city in Europe.

120.   My first is stationed near your heart,
    And serves to brace the mortal frame;
Of young and old it forms a part,
    And to fair woman gives a name.
Who builds a ship must it employ,
    To give it strength to stem the flood,
And Adam felt no real joy
    Till in new form by him it stood.
My second may be long or short,
    Or tight or loose, or wet or dry,
Of cotton, silk, or woolen wrought,
    Of any texture, strength, or dye—
Be made of iron, gold, or steel,
    Of love or hate, of good or ill,
May gently bind, or heavy feel,
    May give support, or rudely kill.
My whole is formed by fashion, skill, and care,
And what few ladies from their dress can spare.

121. How long would a ball be falling, from the top of a tower that was 400 feet high, to the earth?

122. Why are chairs like men?

123. The foot of a ladder 60 feet long remaining in the same place, the top will just reach a window 40 feet high on one side of the street, and another 30 feet high on the other side.   How wide is the street?

124. There is a pile of cannon-balls, the ground tier of which contains 289 balls, and the top tier one ball. Require the whole number of balls in a pile.

125.

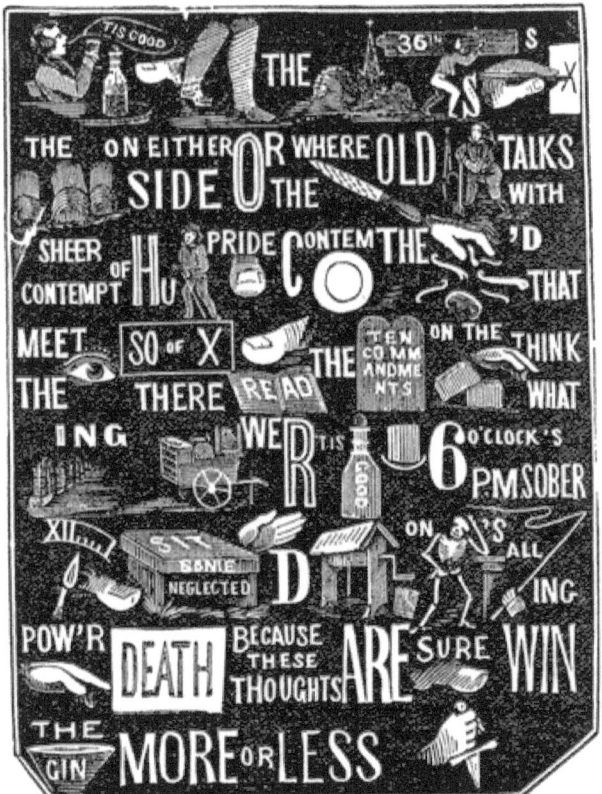

126.

127. What skillful housewife does not know
        When, where to place my first?
      When nicely done, it will not show;
        Conspicuous, it is worst.
      My second all the world must do,
        Either with head or hand,
      In different ways the same pursue,
        On water, or on land.
      My whole a picture is of life,
        Varied with good or ill,
      With bright or dull, with light or dark,
        Arranged with art and skill.

128. What is that which will make you catch cold—
cure the cold—and pay the doctor's bill?

129. Why is a joke like a cocoa-nut?

130. When did Esau, the hairy man, lose his whiskers?

131. Why do postmasters deserve the execration of all
true Americans?

132.   Just equal are my head and tail,
         My middle slender as can be,
       Whether I stand on head or heel,
         'Tis all the same to you or me.
       But if my head should be cut off,
         The matter's true, although 'tis strange,
       My head and body, severed thus,
         Immediately to nothing change

133. If a loafer, smoking a cigar, sets fire to the brush
on his upper lip, is it a case of spontaneous combustion?

134.   liv sin transgre procur damn
       A ing ers   ssion   ed   ation.
         dy Redeem pa purchas   salv

135.

136.

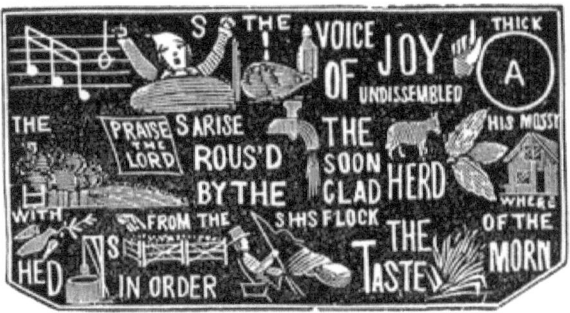

137.

What sailors dread.

9*

138.   I.

Go wide o'er the world,
And everywhere seek me—
In earth, sea, or air,
Thou never shalt meet me !
Go wide o'er the world—
I always am there—
Wherever thou roamest,
In earth, sea, or air !

II.

Go speak to the woodland,
And question of me—
Oh ne'er shalt thou find me,
With forest or tree !
Go, speak to the woodland,
I ever am there,
And live in its whispers,
Though lighter than air !

III.

Go, winnow the wave,
And seek for my breath—
Ah, ocean and river,
Reveal but my death !
Go, winnow the wave,
Tho' with winter it shiver—
There—there shalt thou find
'Mid ocean and river !   [me,

IV.

In whirlwinds I revel,
Yet in zephyrs expire—
I flourish in warmth,
And I perish in fire !
The winter I cherish,
Yet each season I shun ;
Half living in harvest,
In summer, undone !

V.

I come with the warlock—
I go with the ghoul—
I shriek with the wizard—
I hoot with the owl !
I ride on the hazel
Which witches have rent—
I fly on the wing
Which the eagle hath bent.

VI.

I come and I go—
Oft unseen and unsought ;
I live but in words—
I perish in thought.
So to all and to each,
I bid you adieu ;
Yet to all and to each,
I stay double with you !

139. Why is the boy that disturbs a hive like a true Christian ?

140. What is that which has eyes and sees not, ears and hears not, nose and smells not, yet is often regarded as the *beau-ideal* of a human being.

141. Why is the elephant his own servant ?

142. Which of the forest trees bears gain?

143. Who was the heaviest of mechanics?

144. I'm a heavy drag—few things more slow.
Cut off my head, and give me a bow,
And swiftly through the air I go.

145. Why are two heads better than one?

146. Why is a cart-horse always in the wrong place?

147. I follow the plough, and yet I never walk,
Have plenty of teeth, yet neither eat nor talk,
Am strongly barred, and yet I never close,
I scratch and break, but never deal in blows.

148. What is that which has many leaves, but no stem?

149. Why is the letter F like an incendiary?

150. ARITHMETICAL PUZZLE.—This consists of six slips of paper or card, on which are written numbers as expressed in the following columns—

A	B	C	D	E	F
1	2	4	8	16	32
3	3	5	9	17	33
5	6	6	10	18	34
7	7	7	11	19	35
9	10	12	12	20	36
11	11	13	13	21	37
13	14	14	14	22	38
15	15	15	15	23	39
17	18	20	24	24	40
19	19	21	25	25	41
21	22	22	26	26	42
23	23	23	27	27	43
25	26	28	28	28	44
27	27	29	29	29	45
29	30	30	30	30	46
31	31	31	31	31	47
33	34	36	40	48	48
35	35	37	41	49	49
37	38	38	42	50	50
39	39	39	43	51	51
41	42	44	44	52	52
43	43	45	45	53	53
45	46	46	46	54	54
47	47	47	47	55	55
49	50	52	56	56	56
51	51	53	57	57	57
53	54	54	58	58	58
55	55	55	59	59	59
57	58	60	60	60	60
59	59	61	61	61	61
61	62	62	62	62	62
63	63	63	63	63	63

The slips being thus prepared, a person is to think of any one of the numbers which they contain, and to give to the expounder of the question those slips in which the number thought of occurs. To discover this number, the expounder has nothing to do but to add together the numbers at the top of the columns put into his hand. Their sum will express the number thought of.

Example.—Thus, suppose we think of the number **14**. We find that this number is in three of the slips, viz., those marked B, C, and D, which are therefore given to the expounder, who, on adding together 2, 4, and 8, obtains 14, the number thought of.

The trick may be varied in the following manner: Instead of giving to the expounder the slips containing the number thought of, these may be kept back, and those in which the number does not occur be given. In this case, the expounder must add together, as before, the numbers at the top of the columns, and subtract their sum from 63. The remainder will be the number thought of.

The slips containing the columns of numbers are usually marked with letters on the back, and not above the columns, as we have expressed them. This renders the deception more complete, as the expounder, knowing beforehand the number at the top of each column, has only to examine the letters at the back of the slips given him, when he performs the problem without looking at the numbers, and thus renders the trick more extraordinary.

151.   A pair of little quadrupeds,
    Transpose them, and you'll find
The lords of ocean, or the aids
    For disciplining mind ;
Or that which cheers the midnight **hour,**
    Or gilds the flagstaff high ;
Now test your transposition power,
    And for the answer try.

152. When is a chair like a rich lady's dress?

153. One *p*, one *i*, four *a*'s, two *r*'s, two *s*'s, two *t*'s—what do they make, and who has made a fortune by them !

154. What odd number will give, on being divided, a half clear of a fraction ?

155.   I'm in the book, but not on any leaf;
         I'm in the mouth, but not in lip or teeth ;
         I'm in the atmosphere, but never in the air ;
         I wait on every one, but never on a pair ;
         I am with you wherever you may go ;
         And every thing you do I'm sure to know ;
         Though when you did it I should not be there,
         Yet when 'twas done, you'd find me in the chair.

156. What is the difference between Joan of Arc and Noah's ark ?

157. I am composed of seventeen letters.
     My 4, 6, 10, is what we all do.
      "   5, 8, 14, 11, is a great part of the body.
      "   1, 13, 9, 15, is the name of a fish.
      "   7, 16, 2, 10, is a part of speech.
      "   13, 8, 3, is the name of a fowl.
      "   6, 15, 14, is a girl's name.
      "   17, 6, 10, 15, is very useful to vessels.
      "   13, 6, 12, is a personal pronoun.
     My whole is what we may all expect if we live.

158. My first is an instrument, which, though small. has more power than any monarch on earth. It is the lover's friend and the poet's pride ; yet has overthrown kingdoms, ruined reputations, set folks together by the ears, and caused more destruction than plagues, pestilence, or famine. My second, though not quite so mischievous, is very destructive when in improper hands. and my whole, though employed against my first, is deemed its friend and improver.

LEAP FROG.

159. This is a most excellent pastime. It should be played in a spacious place, out of doors, if possible, and the more there are engaged in it, provided they be of the same height and agility, the better is the sport. We will suppose a dozen at play :—Let eleven of them stand in a row, about six yards apart, with all their

faces in one direction, arms folded, or their hands resting on their thighs, their elbows in, and their heads bent forward, so that the chin of each rests on his breast, the right foot advanced, the back a little bent, the shoulders rounded, and the body firm. The last begins the sport by taking a short run, placing his hands on the shoulders of the nearest player, and leaping with their assistance—of course, springing with his feet at the same time—over his head, as represented in the cut. Having cleared the first, he goes on to the second, third, fourth, fifth, etc., in succession, and as speedily as possible. When he has gone over the last, he goes to the proper distance, and places himself in position for all the players to leap over him in their turn. The first over whom he passed, follows him over the second, third, fourth, etc. ; and when he has gone over, the one who begun the game places himself in like manner for the others to jump over him. The third follows the second, and so on until the parties are tired.

160. His heart was sad, and his foot was sore,
When a stranger knocked at the cottager's door;
With travel faint, as the night fell down,
He had missed his way to the nearest town,
And he prayed for water to quench his thirst,
And he showed his purse as he asked for my *first.*
The cotter was moved by the stranger's tale,
He spread the board, and he poured the ale:
" The river," he said, " flows darkly down
Betwixt your path and the lighted town,
And far from hence its stream is crossed
By the bridge on the road that you have lost;
Gold may not buy, till your weary feet
Have traversed the river and reached the street,
The thing you ask; but the wandering moon
Will be out in the sky with her lantern soon;
Then cross o'er the meadow, and look to the right,
And you'll find my *second* by her light."
My *second* shone like a silver floor,
When the traveler passed from the cotter's door;
He saw the town on its distant ridge,
Yet he sighed no more for the far-off bridge;
And his wish of the night soon gained its goal,
For he found my *first* when he reached my whole.

161. What two letters of the alphabet make a prophet?

162. I 8 0 $\frac{M}{\text{day.}}$

163. Plant an orchard of twenty-one trees, so that there shall be nine straight rows, with five trees in each row, the *outline* a regular geometrical figure, and the trees all at unequal distances from each other.

164. B 0 yy $\frac{\text{nor}}{\text{nice}}$ for U c what a fool u b.

165. What part of the horse resembles you?

166. Why is a horse like the prophet Elijah?

167. Why is a new married man like a horse?

168. Why is it profitable to keep fowl?

169. My first is a collection of water; my second is used when speaking of myself; my third is a fruit; my whole is a town in Hindostan.

170. "Thomas," said Charles, "you are good at figures, please give me a *figurative* answer to this question:—What ought one to do who arrives at a friend's house too late for dinner?"

Thomas, after thinking a little, wrote the following—1028,40. What was his meaning?

171. A teacher, having fifteen young ladies under her care, wished them to take a walk each day of the week. They were to walk in five divisions of three ladies each but no two ladies were to be allowed to walk together twice during the week. How could they be arranged to suit the above conditions?

172. My first is a letter, an insect, a word,
    That means to exist; it moves like a bird.
    My next is a letter, a small part of man,
    'Tis found in all climes; search where you can.
    My third is a something seen in all brawls.
    My next you will find in elegant halls.
    My last is the first of the last part of day,
    Is ever in earnest, yet never in play.
    My whole gives a light, by some men abhorred,
    The blessings from which no pen can record.

173. What number is that, which, added separately to 100 and 164, shall make them perfect squares?

174. Why is the letter F like death?

175. Why are mortgages like burglars?

176.   I'm composed of letters four,
    A turkey, cock, or hen;
  Behead me, and I upward soar.
    Put on my head again,
  Transpose me, then a beast I am,
    Both bloodthirsty and wild,
  That preys on many a helpless lamb,
    And oft devours a child.

177. I am a word of three letters, signifying to spoil or injure. Transposed, I am an animal. Transposed again, I am a part of the human frame.

178. Why is a grist-mill like the court-martial which cashiered Fremont?

179. I have wings, yet never fly—
    I have sails, yet never go—
  I can't keep still, if I try,
    Yet forever stand just so.

180. Why is a grist-mill like an orange-tree?

181. What Scripture character was a stupid sheep?

182. What animal that always has a cold chin is used to keep the ladies' chins warm?

183. What two reasons why a young lady going to the altar is certainly going wrong?

184. Why is it dangerous for a teetotaler to have more than two reasons for the faith that is in him?

185. What is the most cheerful part of an arsenal?

186. When does the tongue assume the functions of the teeth ?

187. My first is company, my second is without company, and my third calls company.

188.   An emblem of stupidity,
         My first in forests found ;
       Up in air oft rises high,
         Though fastened to the ground,
       But by sharp means it is removed,
         And managed various ways ;
       By art or skill may be improved,
         Or, perhaps, it makes a blaze.
       My second is of every kind,
         Is good, or bad, or gay ;
       Is dull or bright, to suit all minds,
         By night as well as day.
   The patient seaman keeps with care my whole,
     And well it knows his secrets night and day ;
   And though it has no tongue, nor heart, nor soul,
     It tells the story of the ship's long way.

189. There is a word of six letters. Take off three letters at either end, and add another letter, and it will make one of the most useful members of the body.

190.   Tell me why is it, if you lend
         But forty dollars to a friend,
       It does your kindness more commend
       Than if five hundred you should send ?

191. What is that which is less tired the longer it runs?

192. Why is a tailor finishing your pants like a polite host serving his guests with water-fowl ?

193. What was a month old at Cain's birth, that is not five weeks old now ?

194. What looks worse on a lady's foot than a darned stocking?

195. Which of the girls can answer questions best?

196. What is the shape of a kiss?

197. My first is a busy industrious thing,
Without which no bundle your porter can bring ;
My second is nothing to speak of, yet stands
For thousands and millions, in money or lands ;
My third is a question we meet every day,
Relating to things we do, think, or say ;
My whole is the questioner—once it was you,
If not, 'twas your brother, or cousin, or—whew !
It was somebody else whom your grandmother knew.

198. I am composed of four letters.   We do not 4 2 3,
1 4 2 3, 2 3, 3 4 2.

199. My first is a preposition.
  "   second implies more than one.
  "   third is a pronoun.
  "   fourth some people do not pay.
  "   whole is not consistent.

200. I am a word of four letters often used in prayer.
  Transposed, I become what every one professes.
  Transposed again, I become an adjective, the qual-
    ities of which every one despises.
  Transposed again, I am part of a horse.

201.   My first is poison, slow yet sure,
      That preys on many frames;
    Compounded oft of things impure,
      And called by many names.
    My first and second form my whole,
      That's one of Satan's dens;
    Many a man has lost his soul,
      Through meeting there with friends.

202. I am a word of four letters—the name of a Cape.
  Transposed, I am a portion of the earth's surface.
  Transposed again, I am a kind of meat.
  Transposed again, I become a verb signifying to
    wash.

203. I prove 2 = 1, thus :—
    $x = a$; then $x^2 = ax$
    $x^2 - a^2 = ax - a^2$
    $(x + a)(x - a) = a(x - a)$
    $x + a = a$
    $2 a = a$
    $2 = 1$
  Who will detect the fallacy !

204. In what ship, and in what capacity, do young ladies like to engage?

205. Ethereal thing, on unseen wing,
   Through space my first is wandering;
   It nothing sees, it nothing knows,
   Yet all that's known and seen it shows.
   Brick, iron, mud, stone, reed, or wood,
   My second in all climes has stood—
   A lodge, a nest, where love may rest,
   Or a prison, gloomy, dark, unblest.
   Away on the bleak and desolate peak
   Where the rude tempests howl and shriek,
   Like a friendly eye, looking out from the sky.
   My whole to the wanderer gleams on high.

206. What kind of a ship did Solomon object to?

207. There are two numbers whose product added to
the sum of their squares is 109, and the difference of
whose squares is 24.

208.   In every hedge my second is,
          As well as every tree,
        And when poor school-boys act amiss,
          It often is their fee.
        My first likewise is always wicked,
          Yet ne'er committed sin,
        My total for my first is fitted,
          Composed of brass or tin.

209. My first is a pronoun; my second is not high;
my third we must all do; my fourth is a pronoun of mul-
titude; my whole is musical.

210. What is the difference between a grandmother
and her infant grandchild?

211. Add one to nine and make it twenty.

212. What is that which the dead and living do at the
same time?

213. When winter months have passed away,
          And summer suns shine bright,
        You ope the coffer where I lay,
          And bring my first to light.
        My second is a valiant knight,
          Who wears his crest and spur,
        And when he's challenged to a fight,
          He does not long demur.
        My whole. as ancient fables say,
          Was once a friend of Juno,
        In dress he makes a great display—
          His name by this time you know.

214. Why is a bullet like a tender glance?

215. When innocence first had its dwelling on earth,
     In my first's lovely form it alighted ;
   And still to this time, from the hour of its birth,
     In my first it has greatly delighted.
   My second's a part of a smart lady's dress,
     Yet on age it may also be found ;
   Again, 'tis a garb when the heart feels distress—
     And my whole does with pleasure abound.

216. Why are children at play like a bird in her nest ?

3

217. My first is male or female, young or old,
     ' Tis very sad if you are forced to doubt one;
Much must we pity the false heart or cold,
     Who is so selfish as to live without one.
My second is a noble work of art,
     Which brings together distant shores and lands;
Though neither feet it has, nor head, nor heart,
     'Tis often furnished with a hundred hands.
My whole in youth or age, sickness or health,
     In joy or sorrow, charms to life can give;
Without it, all in vain are hoards of wealth,
     By it unblest in solitude we live.

218. What spice are the Hindoos fond of?

219. Why is a dog like a tanner?

220. Why are A B's successors seedy?

221. What is nothing good for?

222. I am composed of four letters—the initials of four of the principal personages in Europe—the name of a river in Russia; transposed, I am a part of the Crystal Palace; transposed again, I am not *proud*, although elevated above the heads of most people.

223. My first is when the summer wind
     Sweeps rustlingly through the trees,
When the jasmine spray and the eglantine
     Are swayed by the whispering breeze;
My second, a weapon of bloody strife,
     Of steel, so cruel and cold,
Which ruthlessly takes the soldier's life,
     The cowardly, and the bold;
My whole is a Poet, by every one known,
     So wide is his renown.

224. Why is the letter y like a young spendthrift?

225. Why is memory like the peacock?

226. My first in the garden luxuriantly grows,
Delicious and sweet, as every one knows;
My second a noisy, vain, garrulous thing,
The lord of a harem, as proud as a king;
My whole is still prouder, and seems to rejoice
As much in his tail as he does in his voice.

227. One man said to another, "Give me one of your sheep, and I shall have twice as many as you." The other replied, "No, give me one of yours, and I shall have as many as you." How many had each?

228. Where were potatoes first found?

229. Where did cherries come from?

230. Why is a ship under full sail like Niagara?

231. O'er a mighty pasture go
 Sheep in thousands, silver white;
As to-day we see them, so
 In the oldest grandsire's sight.
They drink—never waning old—
 Life from an unfailing brook;
There's a shepherd to their fold,
 With a silver-horned crook.
From a gate of gold let out,
 Night by night he counts them over;
Wide the field they rove about,
 Never hath he lost a rover:
True the dog that helps to lead them,
 One gay ram in front we see;
What the flock, and who doth lead them,
 Sheep and shepherd, tell to me?

232. I am a word of four letters. Take off my hat, and you have something which you do every day. Take off my head, and you have a preposition. Leave off my head and put on my hat, and you have something used before a door. Entire, and taken backward, with my two middle letters transposed, I am a very convenient thing. I, myself, am often eaten.

233. What part of a ship was Cain?

234. What animal resembles the sea, and why?

235. What animal is the most windy, and why?

236. What animal is like an apothecary?

237. What animal is like a stone-breaker?

238. A man had a bar of lead that weighed 40 lbs., and he divided it into four pieces in such a way as to allow him to weigh any number of pounds from one to forty How did he manage the matter?

239. What is the best key to a good dinner?

240. Why is a farm-yard like a hotel?

241. If a woman stands behind a tree, how does the tree stand?

242. Wherein does a turkey-cock differ from a lady?

243. Three men buy a grindstone, 40 inches in diameter, on equal shares. Each one is to use it until he has worn away his share. How many inches in diameter must each one use?

244. What two letters of the alphabet do children like best?

245. Why are Cashmere shawls like deaf persons?

246. Ye mortals—wonder! I'm an elf,
    A strange, mysterious thing;
More powerful than all the sprites
    Within a magic ring.
I speak—although I have no tongue—
    I speak, and thrill the soul;
I sing—and many a song I've sung
    Resounds, while ages roll.
I am a weapon, strong and keen,
    All made of glittering steel;
But human souls—not senseless flesh—
    My sharp two-edges feel.
The greatest writer e'er was born—
    But, ah!—a thievish elf;
For what I write is not, alas!
    Original with myself.
I often take a cooling bath;
    But, like the Ethiop's skin,
When I have bathed, I'm blacker still
    Than when I did begin!
Most kind am I; I glad the heart
    Of many a wretched wight,
And many a sufferer is by me
    Transported with delight.
Most cruel I; I've pierced the soul
    With cutting, burning darts;
I've dashed the fondest hopes to earth,
    I've crushed the lightest hearts.
Yet wise and powerful as I am,
    A very slave am I;
I'm forced the mandates to obey
    Of both the low and high.
Now, witty brains, tell who this is,
    Who blesses and who curses;
Who has no hands, yet still who is
    The writer of these verses.

247. Why is an Indian like a flirt?

248. Why is an Indian like a scholar?

249. How much silk is required to make a spherical balloon, 16 inches in diameter, without allowing for seams?

250. All children love to go to sea, and why?

251. That gentle picture dost thou know,
　　　Itself, its hues, and splendor gaining?
Some change each moment can bestow,
　　　Itself as perfect still remaining;
It lies within the smallest space,
　　　The smallest framework forms its girth,
And yet that picture can embrace
　　　The mightiest objects known on earth:
Canst thou to me that crystal name
　　　(No gem can with its worth compare)
Which gives all light, and knows no flame?
　　　Absorbed is all creation there!
That ring can in itself inclose
　　　The loveliest hues that light the heaven,
Yet from its light more lovely goes
　　　Than all which to it can be given!

252. From 6 take nine, from 9 take 10;
     From 40 take 50, and 6 remain.

253. Why is marriage like truth?

254. Required to divide 45 in four parts, so that the first part with two added, the second with two subtracted, the third divided by two, the fourth multiplied by two, shall equal each other.

255. Where was Major Andre going when he was captured?

256. There is a mansion, vast and fair,
     That doth on unseen pillars rest;
No wanderer leaves the portals there,
     Yet each how brief a guest!
The craft by which that mansion rose,
     No thought can picture to the soul;
'Tis lighted by a lamp which throws
     Its stately shimmer through the whole.
As crystal clear, it rears aloof
     The single gem which forms its roof,
And never hath the eye surveyed
     The master who that mansion made.

257. Why is a sculptor like a man who "splits his sides with laughter?"

258. Why were the Scribes and Pharisees like a great conflagration?

259. My first is a collection of water, my second is used when speaking of myself, my third is a fruit, my whole is a town in Hindostan.

260. X U R, X U B,
     X, 2 X U R 2 me.

261. Why was Daniel like Nebuchadnezzar's image?

SEE-SAW.

262. Several things are necessary to make this sport safe and pleasant. *First*, a strong bar on which to balance your board or plank. *Secondly*, a strong, straight-grained board or plank, which will not crack nor twist. *Thirdly*, an equal weight at each end, or nearly so. *Fourthly*, a clear head, and a steady hand, or foot, to keep up an even motion. With these all right, you will go up and down as easily and smoothly as men of business do, or political parties;—but, hallo there, boys, John has tumbled off, and you will have a smash at the other end, which will leave John's partner in doubt whether he is up or down.

263. What island in the Pacific is always at this sport?

264. What is there at the same time philosophical and ungrammatical in this sport?

265. Why is an elephant like a lady's veil?

3*

266. I was before the world begun,
  Before the earth, before the sun ;
  Before the moon was made, to light
  With brighter beams the starry night ;
  I'm at the bottom of the sea,
  And I am in immensity;
  The daily motion of the earth
  Dispels me, and to me gives birth ;
  You can not see me if you try,
  Although I'm oft before your eye ;
  Such is my whole.   But, for one part,
  You'll find in taste I'm rather tart ;
  Now I become the abode of men—
  And now, for groveling beasts, a pen ;
  I am a man who lives by drinking ;
  Anon I keep a weight from sinking ;
  To take me, folks go far and near ;
  I am what children like to hear ;
  I am a shining star on high ;
  And now, its pathway through the sky ;
  My strength o'erpowers both iron and steel ;
  Yet oft I'm left behind the wheel ;
  I'm made to represent a head ;
  Am found in every loaf of bread ;
  Such are the many forms I take,
  You can not count all I can make ;
  Yet, after all, so strange am I,
  Soon as you know me, then I die.

267. Henry is four feet high and William is five. The sum of their heights multiplied by five is equal to their father's age, plus fifteen.   How old was their father?

268. My first is the name of a river, my second is a pleasant beverage, my third is what we are too apt to do, and my whole is the name of an ancient city.

DEAF AND DUMB ALPHABET.

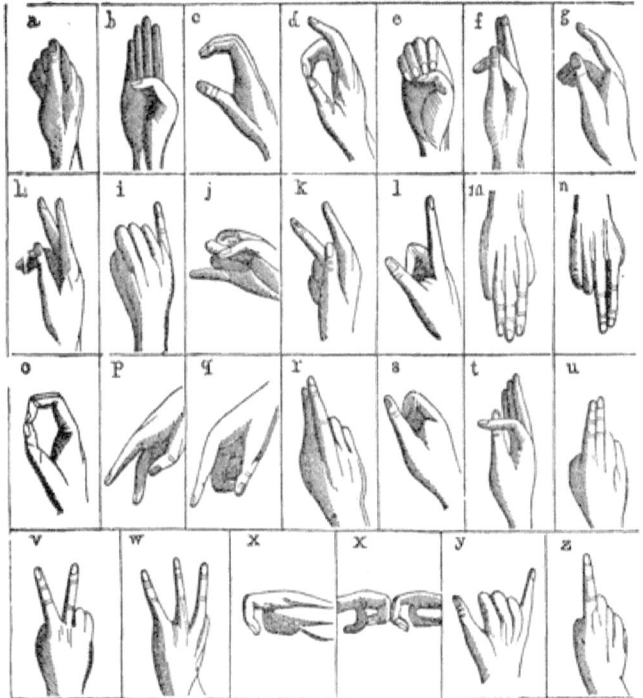

SINGLE HANDED ALPHABET.

269. The deaf and dumb converse with each other, and with their teachers, by signs made with their hands. There are two ways of making the letters with the fingers; in one, both hands are used; in the other, only one. Above, you see how the letters are made with one hand.

270. When are the letters like the keys of a piano?

271. Up and down two buckets ply
    A single well within;
While the one comes full on high,
    One the deeps must win.
Full or empty, never ending,
    Rising now, and now descending,
Always while you quaff from this,
    That one lost in the abyss,
From that well the waters living
    Never both together giving.

272. Come from my first—ay, come! the battle dawn
    is nigh,
And the screaming trump and thundering drum are call-
    ing thee to die!
Fight as thy father fought, fall as thy father fell;
Thy task is taught, thy shroud is wrought, so forward,
    and farewell!
Toll ye, my second, toll! Fill high the flambeau's light,
And sing the hymn of a parted soul beneath the silent
    night;
The wreath upon his head, the cross upon his breast,
Let the prayer be said, and the tear be shed—so take
    him to his rest.
Call ye my whole—ay, call the lord of lute and lay,
And let him greet the sable pall with a noble song to-
    day;
Go, call him by his name! no fitter hand may crave
To light the flame of a soldier's fame on the turf of a
    soldier's grave.

273. Once in a minute, twice in a moment, once in a
man's life?

274. A man said "I lie." Did he lie, or did he tell
the truth?

275. Why is the butcher's dog in the parlor like your mother receiving strange company?

276. Why should a hound never be admitted into the house?

277. Why is your favorite puppy like a doll?

278. How can a person live eighty years, and see only twenty birthdays?

279. What is the difference between twenty four quart bottles, and four and twenty quart bottles?

280. How will you arrange four 9's so as to make one hundred?

281. Amid the serpent race is one
    That earth did never bear;
In speed and fury there be none
    That can with it compare.
With fearful hiss—its prey to grasp—
    It darts its dazzling course,
And locks in one destroying clasp
    The horseman and the horse.
It loves the loftiest heights to haunt—
    No bolt its prey secures;
In vain its mail may valor vaunt,
    For steel its fury lures!
As slightest straw whirled by the wind,
    It snaps the starkest tree;
It can the might of metal grind,
    How hard soe'er it be!
Yet ne'er but once the monster tries
    The prey it threats to gain:
In its own wrath consumed it dies,
    And while it slays is slain.

282. A went to a shoemaker, B, and ordered a pair of boots. At the time appointed for their completion, A called for his boots. The price was $5. A gave B a 20 dollar note, which, not being able to change, he went to C, who gave him four $5 notes. B gave A three of the notes, and kept one. The next day C came to B and told him his $20 note was a counterfeit. B gave C four $5 notes, three of which he borrowed from D. How much did B lose by the operation?

283. When a boy falls, what does he fall against?

284. When he is caught stealing, what does he catch?

285. How many feet ought a thief to have?

286. Why is Tom Tumbledown like Adam when he saw the apple?

287. A friend asserted to me a day or two since, that forty horses only had eighty-four legs. How did it come?

A RIDDLE WITHIN A RIDDLE.

288. Moce ye inugeison nose hist dilerd suesg
Ti si ton cufidlift ouy liwl socfens,
Thaw si hatt burmen—hiwhc fi ouy ivdedi,
Ouy hent liwl hington veale no theire dies?

289. Our family is large, but not much more than one third as large as that of Jacob when he went to live in Egypt. But, like the family of that ancient patriarch, we often migrate to other countries. We do not keep together, whether at home or abroad; we are scattered about in every direction,—at once masters, servants, and slaves to forty-four millions of people. Not a book is printed without our aid; and, what is stranger still, we are all found at the same time in every book in every library and country where the English language is spoken; and on almost every page. Sometimes, though rarely, two of us stand side by side. It is still more rare for us all to appear together arranged in the same order. Nothing is more common with people than to place us in *rows* or *platoons;* but whether in militia, army, or navy—for some of us are employed in all these—we are seldom arranged twice alike. Sometimes one of us stands first; sometimes another. Sometimes a row or platoon consists of only two or three of us; at others of many more; and occasionally of twelve, fifteen, or twenty; and, strangest to relate of all, we can be so placed as to make out about 50,000 rows, no two of which will be exactly alike. Must we not, then, be a useful family? And what, think you, is our *family* name?

290. | | | | | |. Add five more marks to these six, so as to make nine.

291. What tree is that, which has twelve branches, thirty leaves on each branch, and each leaf white on one side, and black on the other?

292. 1. What is the sociable tree? 2. And the dancing tree?
3. And the tree which is nearest the sea?
4. And the busiest tree? 5. The most yielding tree?
6. And the tree where ships may be?
7. The languishing tree? 8. The least selfish tree?
9. And the tree that bears a curse?
10. The chronologist tree? 11. The fisherman's tree?
12. And the tree like an Irish nurse?
13. What's the traitor's tree? 14. And the tell-tale tree?
15. And the tree that is warmest clad?
16 The layman's tree? 17. The housewife's tree?
18 And the tree that makes one sad?
19. What the tree that in death will benight you?
20. And the tree that your wants will supply?
21 And the tree that to travel invites you?
22. And the tree that forbids you to die?
23. What tree do the hunters resound to the skies?
24 What brightens your house, and your mansion sustains?
25. What tree urged the Grecians in vengeance to rise
And fight for the victims by tyranny slain? [yon?
26. The tree that will fight? 27 And the tree that obeys

28. And the tree that never stands still?
29. And the tree that got up?   30. And the tree that was lazy?
31. And the tree neither up nor down hill?
32. The tree to be kissed?   33. And the dandiest tree?
34. And what guides the ships to go forth?
35. The unhealthiest tree?   36. And the tree of the people?
37. And the tree whose wood faces the north?
38. The emulous tree?   39. The industrious tree?
40. And the tree that warms mutton when cold?
41. The reddish-brown tree?   42. The reddish-blue tree?
43 And what each must become ere he's old?
44. The tree in a bottle?   45. And the tree in a fog?
46. And the tree that gives the bones pain?
47. The terrible tree when schoolmasters flog?
48. And what mother and child have the name?
49. The treacherous tree?   50. The contemptible tree?
51. And that to which wives are inclined?
52. The tree that causes each townsman to flee?
53. And what round fair ankles they bind?
54. The tree that's entire?   55. And the tree that is split?
56. The tree half given to doctors when ill?
57. The tree we offer to friends when we meet?
58. And the tree we may use as a quill?
59 The tree that's immortal?   60. The trees that are not?
61 And the trees that must pass through the fire?
62. The tree that in Latin can ne'er be forgot,
    And in England we all must admire?
63. The Egyptian plague tree?   64. And the tree that is dear?
65. And what round itself doth intwine?
66 The tree that in billiards must ever be near?
67. And the tree that by cockneys is turned into wine?

293. Which of the planets would the tortoise like best to live in?

294. Why is a picture surrounded by books like a happy man?

295. Mother sent Mary for an evergreen. The gardener brought a holly. Mary pointed to the sky, and the gardener brought what she wanted. What did Mary mean?

296. When the day breaks, what becomes of the fragments?

297. Novus vir bonus vir ivit ad caudam vel habere suam vestem homines mortuos.

298. EE Marriage EE.

299. What bird is that which has no wings?

300. Add something to 9 to make it less.

301. Why is Satan on a shed like a bankrupt?

302. How is it that trees put on their summer dresses, without opening their trunks?

303. Of three words make one, by the insertion of a single letter.

304. Of a word of one syllable, make a word of three syllables, by the addition of a single letter.

305. Ages ago, when Greece was young,
　　　And Homer, blind and wandering, sung;
　　　Where'er he roamed, through street or field,
　　　My first the noble bard upheld;
　　　Look to the new moon for my next,
　　　You'll see it there, but if perplexed,
　　　Go ask the huntsman, he can show
　　　My name—he gives it many a blow;
　　　My whole, as you will quickly see,
　　　Is a large town in Tuscany,
　　　Which ladies soon will recognize—
　　　A favorite head-dress it supplies.

306. Why is an elephant like a chair?

307. Mr. —wood being at the . of king of terrors, 10 mills for his quakers, and who, which and what. They odor for Dr. Juvenile Humanity, [who] ≡ to Dr. Hay preservers, and little devil behold scarlet his assistance; but, B 4 he arrived, the not legally good changed color, and $\frac{taker}{the}$ was ct for.

308. Given the street and the hour, to find at once the number of children in the street.

309. Given the section of the city, to find at once the number of loafers and vagabonds that infest it.

CHRISTMAS TREE.

310. This is a very curious and interesting kind of a tree. It is found, loaded with every variety of strange *fruit,* on tables, bare floors, or carpets. It has no roots, but is most wonderful for its yielding powers, though it bears only once a year, and that always on Christmas Eve. The last one that I saw was at Uncle Hiram Hatchet's. Cousin Hannah thus describes it:

"At last, when none of us expected it, he (Uncle H.) threw open the folding doors, and let us into the little parlor. There was displayed the Christmas tree, in all its glory. Every little twig bore some present; dolls

and doll furniture, pins, ear-rings, bracelets, slippers,
watch-guards and purses, ships, windmills, and beautiful
books, besides all sorts of fruits and bon-bons, and all
blazing with light from the numberless candles that
seemed to grow out of the branches."

> A tree that, without life or root,
>   Without a blossom, bud, or flower,
> Bears various and most precious fruit,
>   That comes and goes in one short hour.

311. My first is an adjective, short and dry,
> Which an absence of moisture seems to imply,
> Or, in reference to mind, that kind of wit,
> Which is slack on the rein, and sharp on the bit
> My second is a sort of hole, or den,
> Unfit for the resort of timid men,
> Whence once the righteous came safely out,
> While the wicked were wholly put to rout.
> My whole is an author of classic fame,
> If you know the man, please tell me his name.

312. What poet do miners value most?

313. What poet is least distinguished for brevity?

314. Which of the English poets would be most likely
to make a lion feel at home?

315. Why were the Amalekites never allowed to
speak?

316. Which of the reptiles is a mathematician?

317. What Scripture character would have made a
suitable husband for a tall laundress?

318. What two syllables of the marriage ceremony are
most interesting to the priest?

319. What part of a house measures about two quarts?

320 When is a door not a door?

321 Why are ladies sitting on the stoop, like an unfinished house?

322. What stone opens and shuts at your convenience?

323.
    Read see how me
    Down will I love
    And you love you
    Up and you if

324. Why is a thing purchased like a shoe?

325. Why is a man who makes a wager of a cent, like a person recovering from illness?

326. Why is an unpaid bill like the moisture in the morning?

327. Why is a sanguinary epistle like a surgeon?

328. Ere from the east arose the lamp of day,
Or Cynthia gilt the night with paler ray—
Ere earth was form'd, or ocean knew its place,
Long, long anterior to the human race
I did exist.   In chaos I was found,
When awful darkness shed its gloom around.
In heaven I dwell, in those bright realms above,
And in the radiant ranks of angels move.
But when th' Almighty, by his powerful call,
Made out of nothing this stupendous ball,
I did appear, and still upon this earth
Am daily seen, and every day have birth.
With Adam I in Paradise was seen,
When the vile serpent tempted Eve to sin;
And, since the fall, I with the human race
Partake their shame and manifest disgrace.
In the dark caverns of old ocean drear
I ever was, and ever shall appear.
In every battle firmly I have stood,   [blood.
When plains seem lav'd, whole oceans dy'd with
But, hold—no more! It now remains with you
To find me out and bring me forth to view.

329. Why is a lost child like you?

330. Why is Fremont equal to eight honest politicians?

331 How did Jonah feel when the whale swallowed him?

332. Why were the Hebrews called sheep?

333. Why is it dangerous to flirt in a hay-field?

334. Under what tree is it most proper to make love?

335. Under what shade can you dance best?

336. Why is a dashing young buck a favorite with the ladies?

337. 1. I am constantly in the midst of money. 2. I am continually putting people in possession of property. 3. I increase the number of most things that come in my way. 4. I am no friend to the distressed needlewomen, for I render needles unnecessary. 5. Yet whenever I undertake a dress, I infallibly make it sit. 6. I am quar-

4

relsome, for a word and a blow is my maxim.　7. In fact,
with me a word becomes a weapon.　8. And merriment
becomes slaughter.　9. It is commonly remarked that
drink converts men into swine, but I transform wine
itself into the same animals.　10. Deprived of me, certain
railway speculations come out in their true character
11. A team can draw a wagon well without me, still,
when I am in front, the speed is wonderfully increased.
12. Marvelous products may be obtained from peat, but
when I am extracted from earth, pure oil alone remains.
13. Let me go before, and a story is sure to be stale.
14. And if I am left out, it will be political.　15. I am
strongly attached to pluralities.　16. With respect to
free trade, I turn corn itself into contempt.　17. I am in
the midst of Russia and Prussia, and abundant among
the Swiss.　18. Were I withdrawn from that unhappy
country, Spain, nothing would be left but grief.　19. After sport, when I take my departure, the evening is often
finished with what remains.　20. At a soiree I am always
in good time.　21. In person I am much bent, though I
was formerly more upright.　22. As to my education, I
was always head of the school.　23. Though invariably
at the bottom of my class.　24. With me age looks wise.
25. But a gentleman is better without me, as accompa-
nied by me he appears feminine.　26. On the contrary,
a lady ought not to part with me, for if she loses me she
seems masculine.　27. I am an unwelcome visitor, for
with me sorrow begins and happiness ends.　28. Sadness
commences, and, 29. Bliss terminates.　30. Yet it is in
my power to transform cares into what is delightful.

338. Nebuchadnezzar's lions were very undevout when
Daniel was with them, and very poetical with his enemies.　Please explain.

339. Why is a hunter like an omnibus pickpocket?

340. Figures, they say, won't lie; but here
Is something either false or queer.
I find that, in my family,
One taken from two still leaves me three,
And two from two, by the same score,
Leaves a remainder of just four.

341. My first is a measure much used in the East,
Or a close-covered vehicle drawn by one beast;
My second is a prefix—a small preposition—
Two thirds of a tavern—a paid politician;
My whole, though part of a vessel, has stood
Alone on the prairie, or 'neath the great wood,
And often is found, poor, wretched, and mean,
The city's proud palaces squatting between.

BLACK-EYED MARY'S ALGEBRAICAL PROBLEM.

342. Take two numbers, such that the square of the first, plus the square of the second, shall equal 8; while the first, plus the product of the first and second, shall equal 6.

N B.—If any choose to work this out algebraically, it will be found to be no trifling puzzle. See MERRY's MUSEUM for 1856.

343. What's that the poor's most precious friend,
 Nor less by kings respected—
Contrived to pierce, contrived to rend,
 And to the sword connected.
It draws no blood, and yet doth wound ;
 Makes rich, but ne'er with spoil ;
It prints, as earth it wanders round,
 A blessing on the soil.
The eldest cities it hath built,
 Bade mightiest kingdom rise ; it
Ne'er fired to war, nor roused to guilt :
 Weal to the states that prize it!

344. When is a political candidate like Samson's guests ?

345. What is the most suitable dance to wind off a frolic ?

346. Revolving round a disk I go
 One restless journey o'er and over ;
The smallest field my wanderings know,
 Thy hand the space could cover :
Yet many a thousand miles are passed
 In circling round that field so narrow :
My speed outstrips the swiftest blast,
 The strongest bowman's arrow.

347. Why are buckwheat cakes like the caterpillar?

348. What relation does the soap-bubble bear to the boy who makes it?

349. Why do girls blow bubbles better than boys?

350. What is the difference between a boy and his shadow?

351. Why is a soap-bubble like Adam?

352. I have no life, yet, as I fly,
    A thing of beauty to the eye,
    I bear, my glittering shape beneath,
    A part of my Creator's breath;
    With ever-changing shade and hue
    I rise and vanish from the view,
    And, though a phantom deemed, I share,
    In portions, water, earth, and air.

353.   I go, but never stir,
    I count, but never write,
I measure and divide, and, sir,
    You'll find my measures right.
I run, but never walk,
    I strike, but never wound,
I tell you much, but never talk,
    In my diurnal round.

354. When a boy falls into the water, what is the first thing he does?

355. How would the proposed removal of the Pope to Jerusalem be a false move for the Papacy, and a true one for the Papal States?

356. Why is a coachman a generous man?

357. Why is a dog like a clock-maker's safe?

358. Why is the cook more noisy than a gong?   ·

359. Describe a partisan, and answer a question in the · same words.

360.   A word of one syllable call to your mind,
The letters of which will, if rightly combined,
Provide you with two kinds of fuel—ay, more,
A warm piece of clothing—and fasten your door.

361.   Let two Roman fives at extremities meet.
At the right hand of these, add two circles complete;
Then five times one hundred place at the right hand,
And a nice winter's comfort they make as they stand.

362. What number is that which can be divided by 2, 3, 4, 5, and 6, leaving, in each case, a remainder of 1, and by 7, without a remainder?

363. How long ago were trunks first used?

364 I'm black or white, I in brown or gray,
I'm tall or flat, I'm grave or gay,
As soft as wool, or stiff as tin,
A nest for wits to nestle in.
I hold great intellects, yet oft
Am bothered with the weak and soft,
And sometimes crusty, hard, and thick,
They fill me with we' burned brick.
Fashion controls me, yet I wear
Some aspects to make fashion stare.
Though always for one place designed,
I change as often as the wind.

I'm dumb, and yet, in spite of that,
Make more than half of every " Chat,"
I'm mild—yet none can hate—(don't doubt **me**)
Nor raise a fighting-cock without me.

365. In every home I stand confessed,
    A friend of quiet, peace, and rest;
    Take off my head, and on your head
    My streamers rise, black, brown, or red;
    Cut now again, and take my neck off,
    You leave my substance not a speck of,
    But, with ethereal lightness gay,
    I pass in idle breath away.

366. What relation is the door-mat to the scraper?

367. In what do grave and gay people differ at church?

368. What sea would make the best sleeping-room?

369. 'Tis said of lawyers Grab and Clinch,
    They take an ell when you offer an inch;
    But I can do a smarter thing—
    Give me an ell, I will make it ring;
    If for advice you come to me
    When you are ill, I call for the fee;
    If any road you chance to wend,
    You think you've reached the very end,
    I come and give it such a turn,
    You find there's something yet to learn;
    If to the inn you seek for rest,
    I chuck you in a box or chest;
    The beggar's rags I make so proud,
    He of his garments boasts aloud;
    The aged and infirm with me
    Lose caution and timidity;
    For, young or old, to every one
    I furnish, if not muscle, bone.

370. Why is a spotted dog most reliable?

371. In what does a dog differ from a groom in his treatment of a horse?

372. One of a gallant vagrant band,
    My name is known in every land;
    In all earth's changes I am there;
    Without me none may war declare,
    Or treat of peace, or try their parts
    On manufacture, tillage, arts;
    By me a patient saint of old
    Was changed into a warrior bold;
    I made old Abner's father near;
    His wife was deaf, I made her hear;
    His house I put upon his back;
    His jaw an iron bond I make;
    Bad spirit by my presence claims
    To be the end of human aims;
    And a young bear is seen to be
    A coveted jewel of the sea.

4*

373. *Problem.*—To make a restless child quiet and contented.

374. *Problem.*—To teach a child to be honest, industrious, and useful.

375. Why is Merry's Museum like a note falling due?

376. I consist of eleven letters.

My 9th, 7th, and 1st, is where infants often repose;
    " 3d, 10th, and 7th, is a foreign plant much used by us;
    " 1st, 7th, 5th, 9th, 4th, and 11th, is to treat by word of mouth;
    " 6th, 4th, 7th, and 8th, is a delicious fruit;
    " 2d, 7th, and 3d, to do which affords great satisfaction;
    " 4th, 7th, and 5th, is an essential part of the head;
    " 3d, 10, 7th, and 8th, is often used for joy or sorrow;
    " whole is the name of a distinguished writer for Merry's Museum.

377. Why is Merry's Museum like a good wife?

378. I am composed of twelve letters.

W. 2, all 6, 2, 10, with 10, 5, 2, 9, which a 12, 8, 1, 7, 5, i, 6, 6, 11, 4, 10, not to have, and which a 3, 8, 1, 12, 5, 9, 11, 4, 2, l. 5, 12, i. 6, 11, 9, 2, 6.

379. Why is Merry's Museum like a good mother?

380. What was the difference—can you show—
Between the Prodigal in his woe,
 And Lazarus, in his low estate,
Feeding on crumbs at Dives' gate?

381. What fish does a bride wear on her finger?

382. Why is Merry's Museum like a printing-office?

ANSWERS TO PUZZLES.

1. THE rose shall cease to blow,
   The eagle turn a dove,
The stream shall cease to flow,
   Ere I will cease to love.
The sun shall cease to shine,
The world shall cease to move,
The stars their light resign,
   Ere I will cease to love.

2. Short shoes and long corns to the enemies of freedom.

3. The rope-maker.

4. Because they can not be got off without a bow (beau).

5. Because he stops at the sound of wo.

6. One takes the dish with the egg.

7. One, after which his stomach is not empty.

8. The smallest.

9. The first geometrical puzzle is solved in this way—

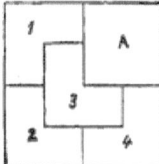

The second puzzle is solved in this way—

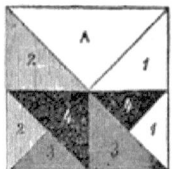

The different colors represent the several sons' portions.

10. The tiger couches in the wood,
    And waits to shed the traveler's blood ;—
        So couch we.
    We spring upon him to supply
    What men unto our wants deny;
        And so springs he.

11. Work, work, work!
    My labor never flags;
    And what are its wages? A bed of straw,
    A crust of bread—and rags,
    That shattered roof—this naked floor,
    A table—a broken chair,
    And a wall so blank, my shadow I thank
    For sometimes falling there!
    With fingers weary and worn,
    With eyelids heavy and red,
    A woman sat in unwomanly rags,
    Plying her needle and thread-

Stitch ! stich ! stitch !
In poverty, hunger, and dirt,
    And still with a voice of dolorous
        pitch.
She sang the "Song of the Shirt."

12. A pack of cards.

13. Striking.

14. Because words are passing between them

15. Footman.

16. Because his is all *net* profit.

17. Because he is surrounded with dues (dews).

18. Adam.

19. Heroine.

20. Spark.

21. Tear.

22. Because it is a bad habit.

23. Because it is felt.

24. Because it is a resting-place for the traveler.

25 There's a grim hearse horse,
    In a jolly round trot,
    To the churchyard a poor man is
        going, I wot.
    The road it is rough,
    And the hearse has no springs,
    And hark to the dirge the sad
        driver sings—
    "Rattle his bones over the stones,
    He's only a pauper, whom no-
        body owns."

26 Of all the birds that e'er I did see,
    The owl is the strangest in every
        degree,
    For all the long day she sits in a
        tree,
    And when the night comes, away
        flies she,
            To whit-to-whoo.
    To whom drinkest thou ?   Sir
        Noodles, to you.

This song is well sung, I make
    you a vow,
And he is a knave that tileth
    now.
Nose, nose, and who gave thee
    that jolly red nose ?
Cinnamon and ginger, nutmeg
    and cloves,
And they gave me my jolly red
    nose.

27. To ashes.

28. Short.

29. Shakespeare.

30. Time.

31. Wallace.

32. Because they are often toasted.

33. Because he is always *for* getting.

34. I, ser.

35. Because he has nothing to boot.

36. Full five hundred years I've hung,
    In my old grey turret high,
    And many a different theme I've
        sung,
    As the hours went winging by.
    I've pealed the chimes of a wed-
        ding morn ;
    Ere night I've sadly tolled to
        say
    That the maid was coming love
        lorn,
    And here I end my lay.

37. The joyful can sing on spirit
        wings
    Each morn his lofty height,
    In rapt'rous notes he sweetly
        sings.
    And hails th' approaching
        light ;
    But I from grief no solace know,
    No portal from the night,
    All joys to me insipid grow,
    Afford me no delight.

38. Because it is often tolled (told)

39. Your name.

40. The letter M.

41. Forty-eight feet.

42. In solving this question it is clear that to pick up the first stone and put it into the basket, the person must walk two yards, one in going for the stone and another in returning with it; that for the second stone he must walk four yards, and so on increasing by two as far as the hundredth, when he must walk two hundred yards, so that the sum total will be the product of 202 multiplied by 50, or 10,000 yards. If any one does not see why we multiply 202 by 50 in getting the answer, we refer him to his arithmetic.

43. Hour-glass.

44. Pen-man-ship.

45. There was a man who was Nott born,
His father was Nott born before him;
He did Nott live, he did Nott die,
And his epitaph is Nott o'er him.

46. Because it is in firm (infirm).

47. To keep his head warm.

48. Hark! the muffled drum sounds the last march of the brave,
The soldier retreats to his quarters, the grave,
Under Death, whom he owns his Commander-in-chief,
No more he'll turn out with the ready relief;
But in spite of Death's terrors or cannon's alarms,
When he hears the last trump he'll stand to his arms!
Farewell! brother soldiers, in peace may you rest,
And light lie the turf on each veteran breast,
Until that review when the souls of the brave

Shall behold the chief ensign, fair mercy's flag, wave;
Then, freed from Death's terrors and hostile alarms,
When we hear the last trump, we'll stand to our arms.

49. Doctor Long expects Dr. Short to explain the misunderstanding between them.

50. To you who live *single*, if this at all trouble you,
My first comes in kindness, commanding to *double you*.
And again, it will *double you*, if, like a clown,
You lift high your *sole*, and bend your head down;
Or, cut it in twain, two *V*'s will appear,
And *V* counting *five*, both make *ten* it is clear.
My second, alas! comes shrouded in gloom,
It is *O*, which makes *wo, the sinner's sad doom.*
Now see what a change comes over the scene,
If my third, which is *O*, be added again.
Now 'tis *woo*—and what bachelor's heart does not beat,
To *woo* a sweet damsel, to keep warm his feet;
To cheer by her smiles his lone hours—and thus
Escape, by good fortune, the bachelor's curse!
My fourth and my last, as I'll go on to tell,
Is nought more or less than a *capital L.*
Now *L* being *fifty*, will even divide
One Hundred, or teachers and books have all lied.
Now examine with care, and plain you will see
That to unlock a secret, an *L* is the key;
For *woo*, with *L* added, is changed into *wool*,
Whether worn on *a sheep*, or an African's skull.

Whether made into clothing, for
  bed or for body,
For "*sage politician*," or some
  other *noddy*.
It is used, the world over, in
  commerce and trade;
But its *last use*, I trow, was to
  make a *charade*.

51.   SONG OF THE SUN.

Not a rose that blooms,
Not a ring that assumes
    The rainbow's beautiful front,
But's indebted to me,
As ye plainly see,
    For the scent or splendor on 't.
The moon and the stars
That around ye roll,
    The systems ye can not discern,
Are warmed by my rays,
And partake of the soul
    And the spirit that in me burn.
And nothing throws back with such
  splendor my rays,
As the sea's mighty mirror in mid-
  summer days.

52. And like the temple of this
body, the cloud-capped towers, the
gorgeous palaces, the solemn temples,
the great globe itself shall fall, and,
like this insubstantial vision faded,
leave not a rack behind.

53. Letter I.

54. When it is a cutter

55. Letter N.

56. Five when peeled.

57. He is a bit of a buck.

58. His daughter.

59. It matures by falling dew.

60 Ben-ha-dad.

61., Because it is never peeled (peal-
ed) but once.

62. Because it is every year doub-
ling (Dublin).

63. Tobacco.

64 The nose

65 Because they have so many
panes (pains).

66 J'ai grand appétit. Allons sou-
per.

67. Water.

68. Ice.

69 Those that come after T.

70. 'Twas at night, when the bell had
        tolled twelve,
      And poor Susan was laid on
        her pillow,
    In her ear whispered some fleet-
        ing elf—
      "Your love is now tossed on
        the billow"
          Far, far at sea.
    All was dark as she woke out of
        breath—
      Not an object her fears could
        discover ;
    All was still as the portals of
        death,
      Save fancy, which painted her
        lover
          Far, far at sea.
    So she whispered a prayer, closed
        her eyes,
      But the phantom still haunted
        her pillow,
    While in terror she echoed his
        cries,
      As struggling he sunk on the
        billow
          Far, far at sea.

71. Lightly tread—'tis holy ground :
    Countless dead hark, hark around ;
    Angel guards their watches keep,
    While frail mortals sink to sleep :
    And the moon, with feeble rays,
    Gilds the stream that bubbling
        plays,
    And murmurs, as soft it flows,
    Music meet for lovers' woes.

72. Eye.

73. Canister.

74. Forte tu, atrox tenes, forti
Sexto Fortinato

75 The forceps pinches, the awl punches.

76. At the peaceful midnight hour,
Every sense and every power
Chained lies in downy sleep ;
Then our careful watch we keep,
While the wolf, in nightly prowl,
Bays the moon with hideous howl ;
Closed are bars, a vain resistance ;
Shrieks are raised, but no assistance ;
Silence ! or you'll meet your fate ;
Your keys. jewels, money, plate.
Locks, bolts, and bars soon fly asunder,
Then to rifle, rob, and plunder.

77. Ad-here.—In-here.—Co-here.

78. Because only the *bony part* is left.

79. He is known by his axe (acts).

80. XII., that is, a cross two i's (across two eyes).

81. Because he kneads (needs) it most.

82. The letter R.

83. The coward skulking round a house,
Is like a mouse-trap as you see,
For that will *puzzle any mouse*,
And *pusillanimous* is he.

84. Green grass is like a mouse, because the cattle eat it (cat 'll eat it).

85. It is not aloud (allowed).
Private earing (privateering) is unlawful.

86. Salt-cellar.

87. Because it is not currant (current).

88. Glorious Apollo from on high beheld us
Wand'ring to find a temple for his praise ;
Sent Polyhymnia hither to shield us
While we ourselves such a temple might raise.
Thus then, Guards, hands and hearts joining,

Sing we in harmony Apollo's praise.
Here every generous sentiment awaking,
Music inspiring our mutual joy,
Each social bumper giving and partaking,
Song and good cheer our time employ.

89. To let you know he is coming.

90. Because of the sand which is (sandwiches) under your feet.

91. Mag-pie.

92. His father was translated.

93. But-ton.

94. A shoe.

95. On ! by the spur of valor goaded,
Pistols primed and rifles loaded,
Courage strikes on hearts of steel.
While each star through the dark gloom of night,
Lends a clear and cheering light,
Who a doubt or fear can feel ?
Now through woods like serpents creeping,
Then on our prey like lions leaping,
Calvert to the onset leads us.
Let the weary traveler dread us.
Struck with terror and amaze ;
While our swords in lightning pouring,
Thunder to our rifles roaring.

96. A bell.

97. $\dfrac{c\,b\,d}{d\,c+c}$ hours to go down.

$\dfrac{2\,a}{b}$ average rate of rowing

$\dfrac{c+b}{d\,c+c}$ hours to go up.

$\dfrac{c\,b}{c+d}$ time up.

$\dfrac{d\,b}{c+d}$ time down

$\dfrac{2\,a}{b}$ miles per hour.

98 The hounds gain 6 rods in every 21 They must therefore run as many times 21 rods as 6 will go into 96. Therefore 96 ÷ 6 = 16. 21 = 336 rods.

99.

100. He wrote s before it, making it six.

101. Live, evil, vile, Levi, veil.

102. When the rosy dawn awaking
  Paints with gold the verdant lawn ;
  Flies, on the wings of time disporting,
  Sip the sweets and taste the dawn.
  Warbling birds the day proclaiming,
  Singing sweet the lively strain;
  They forsake their leafy dwelling,
  To secure the golden grain.
  See ; content the humble gleaner
  Picks the scattered ears that fall.
  Nature, all her children viewing,
  Kindly bounteous cares for all.

103 Musk-melon, if your second is turned inside out; thus, lem-on.

104. Merry's Museum.

105. "Now before you."

106. Pat-ten.

107 Because it is far fetched and full of nonsense

108. Make an impression.

109 Sweet are the roses that bloom by yon fountain,
  And sweet are the cowslips that spangle the grove,
  And sweet is the breeze that blows o'er the mountains ;
  But sweeter by far is the lad that I love.

I'll weave a gay and fresh blooming garland,
  With lilies and roses,
  And sweet, blooming posies,
  To give to the lad my heart tells me I love.

May the brow of the brave never want a wreath of laurel.

110. May the trees of liberty flourish round the globe, and every man partake of its fruit. May the wings of love never lose a feather

111. Prescription--proscription

112. Bar-gain .

113. 1,600 ÷ 32 = 50. $50^2 \times 16$ = 40,000

114. Tanner.

115. Because it makes a *man go.*

116. Hand-el.

117. Wave, thou royal purple stream,
  Gilded by the solar beam
  In my goblet sparkling rise,
  Cheer my heart, and glad mine eyes.
  My spirit mounts on fancy's wing,
  Anointing me a merry king.
  While I live, I'll lave my pipe.
  When I'm dead and gone away.
  Let my drinking partner say
  A month he reigned, but that was ripe.

118. No gems which plumèd fortune wears,
  No drop that hangs from beauty's ears,
  Nor the bright stars which night's blue vault adorn,
  Nor rising suns that gild the vernal morn,
  Shine with such lustre as the tear that breaks
  For other's woe down virtue's manly cheeks.

119. Frankfort-on-the-Maine.

120. Rib-band.

121. $400 \div 16 = 25.$ $\sqrt{25} = 5 -$ five seconds.

122. Because they have arms and legs.

123. $\begin{cases} \sqrt{60} - 30^3 = 51.96152 \\ \sqrt{60} - 40^3 = 44.72136 \end{cases}$
$\qquad\qquad 96.68288.$ *Ans.*

124. 1,785.

125. 'Tis good to tread the church-
 yard's walks,
And mark the graves on either side;
Or where the rough old sexton talks
 With sheer contempt of human
 pride ;
To contemplate the scattered bones
 That meet the eye so often there ;
To read the inscription on the stones,
 And think what fleeting things we
 are.
'Tis good at twilight's sober hour,
 To sit on some neglected tomb,
And dwell on death's all-startling
 power,
And muse upon our certain doom.
Because these thoughts are sure to
 win
 The spirit more or less from sin.

126. Aching teeth are bad tenants.

127. Patch-work.

128. A draft.

129. It is good for nothing till it is cracked.

130. When his brother Jacob shaved him.

131. Because they blacken the face of Washington.

132. The figure 8.

133. Certainly ;—Webster says : "*spontaneous* is applicable to ani-mals destitute of reason."

134 A living sinner's transgres-sion procured damnation.
A dying Redeemer's passion pur-chased salvation.

135. Early to bed, and early to rise,
 Makes a man healthy,
 Wealthy, and wise.

136. Music awakes
The native voice of undissembled
 joy,
And thick around the woodland
 hymns arise.
Roused by the cock, the soon-clad
 shepherd
Leaves his mossy cottage, where
 with peace
He dwells, and from the crowded
 folds in
Order drives his flock, to taste the
 verdure of
The morn.

137. Friday.

138. W.

139. He is an earnest bee-leaver.

140. A portrait.

141. He carries his own trunk.

142. The oak—(a-corn).

143. Ful-ton.

144. Harrow.

145. They are four-sighted (fore-sighted).

146. Because the cart is before the horse.

147. Harrow.

148. A book.

149. Because it makes ire fire.

150. (Arithmetical Puzzle.)

151. Rats—tars—arts—stars.

152. When it is sat-in.

153. Sarsaparilla. Dr. Townsend.

154. XI divided $\frac{\text{VI}}{\text{AI}}$ gives six. IX divided in the same way, gives four.

155. The letter O.

156. The one was Maid of Orleans, the other was made of chittim wood.

157. Sunshine and shadow.

158. Pen-knife.

159. (Leap Frog.)

160. Bed-ford.

161. C—R (Seer).

162. I ate nothing Monday

163.

164. Be not too wise, nor over nice, for you see what a fool you be.

165. The shoe—U.

166. He is fed from a loft.

167. He is bride-led.

168. For every grain they give a peck.

169. Pondicherry.

170. One ought to wait for tes.

171.

```
SUN.   MON.   TUES.  WED.      THUR.  FRI.   SAT.
a b c  s d g  a k n  s e l a h o  a f p  a l m
d e f  b e h  b l o  b f m b l p  b d n  b g k
g h i  c m p  c f t  c g n c d k  c h l  c e o
k l m  f k o  d h m  d l o e m n  e l k  d l p
n o p  i l n  e g p  h k p f g l  g m o  h f n
```

172. Bible.

173. 125.

174. Because without it life is a lie, or it makes life a lie.

175. They secure (seek your) money

176. Fowl, owl, wolf.

177. Mar, ram, arm.

178. It breaks the kernel (colonel)

179. Windmill.

180. Always in flour.

181. Adullam (a dull lamb).

182. The chin-chilla (chilly).

183. She is miss-taken and miss-led.

184. Because three scruples make a dram

185. The ball-room.

186. When it back-bites.

187. Co-nun-drum.

188. Log-book.

189. Hannah—hand

190. It is but D *sent*, as you see,
If you 500 send,
But truly XL *lent* 'twill be,
When you the 40 lend.

191. A wheel.

192. He presses them with a goose

193. The moon.

194. One that needs darning.

195. Ann, sir.

196. Elliptical—a-lip-tickle.

197. B-o-y.

198. Mate—(eat-meat-at-tea)

199. In-co-he-rent.

200. Amen, name, mean, mane.

201. Grog-shop.

202. Vela, vale, veal, lave.

203. Not I.

204. In court-ship, as *marry*-ners.

205. Light-house.

206. Sureti-ship.

207. 5 and 7.

208. Candle-stick.

209. Me-lo-di-ous.

210. The one is careless and happy, the other is hairless and cappy.

211. *IX*—cross the *I*, it makes XX.

212. Lie.

213. Pea-cock.

214. Because it pierces hearts.

215. Child-hood.

216. In earnest (in her nest).

217. Friend-ship.

218. Cayenne (K. N.).

219. He is known by his bark.

220. They are C D.

221. Good for nothing.

222. Neva, nave, vane.

223. Shake-speare.

224. Because it makes Pa-pay.

225. It has eyes behind.

226. Pea-cock.

227. 7 and 5.

228. In the ground.

229. From the tree.

230. Because she shows her flowing sheets.

231. Moon and stars.

232. Meat (eat—at—mat—team).

233. The tiller.

234. The lion, because he roars, and has a flowing mane (main).
Leviathan, because he swallows up the rivers.

235. The bull, because he *bellows*
The whale, because he *blows*.

236. The ass, because he *brays*.
Dr. Pott's horse, because a *Pott he carries*.

237. The rooster, because he *picks* and crows.

238. 1, 3, 9, 27, are the weights of the several pieces.

239. A tur-key.

240. It is generally patronized by gobblers.

241. In the ground.

242. He flourishes his fan behind him.

243. 1st, 7.36. 2d, 9.56. 3d, 23.08.

244. C-and-y—candy.

245. Because we can not make them here (hear).

246. A steel pen.
The weapon's *a steel pen*, I think,
Unless I've made a blunder;
When Hatchet dips it in the ink,
I'd like to stand from under.
" Old lady"—quotha! think of that.
My goodness—heart-alive!
I tell you, Mr. Hatchet—flat!
I'm scarcely sixty-five.

247. He has many cast-off bows (beaux).

248. He is a well re(a)d man.

249. 804,247,552 square inches

250. Because c-and-y spell candy

251. The eye.

252.
$$\begin{array}{cccc} \text{S I X} & \text{I X} & \text{X L} \\ \text{I X} & \text{X} & \text{L} \\ \hline 8 & \text{I} & \text{X} \end{array}$$

253. Because it is a *certain tie* (certainty).

254. 8, 12, 20, 5.

255. To the gallows

256. The earth and firmament.

257. Because he makes faces and busts (bursts).

258. Because they "devoured widows' houses."

259. Found !-cherry.

260. Cross you are, cross you be,
Cross, too cross, you are for me.

261. Because the lions could not eat him.

262. (See-saw.)

263. Hi-lo.

264. It places the present (see) before the past (saw).

265. Because there is a *b* in *both*.

266. *Obscurity*, in which may be found sour, city, sty, sot, buoy, tour, story, orb, orbit, rust, rut, bust, crust.

267. He was 30 years old.

268. Exe-te-r.

269. (Deaf and dumb alphabet.)

270. When they are fingered.

271. Day and night.

272. Camp bell.

273. The letter M.

274. If he told the truth, he lied; if he lied, he told the truth.
He lied. If he did lie, he would not say so

275. He is a ma' stiff.

276. He *chases* the deer (dear) and is never chased (chaste).

277. Because he is a pup-pet.

278. He must be born on the 29th of February.

279. 56 quarts difference.

280. $99\frac{9}{8}$

281. Lightning.

282. $15, and boots.

283. Against his will.

284. A whipping.

285. $16\frac{1}{2} = $ a rod.

286. He is about to fall.

287. Forty horses have 80 *fore* legs.

288. Come, ye ingenious ones, this riddle guess,
It is not difficult, you will confess.
What is that number which, if you divide,
You then will nothing leave on either side?
The number –8–

289. The alphabet.

290. **N I N E.**

291. The year, 12 months, 30 days, night and morning, black and white.

292. 1. The Tea tree.
2. Hop vine.
3. Beech.
4. Bee.
5. India-rubber.
6. Bay.
7. Pine.
8. Yew (You, not I).
9. Fig.
10. Date.
11. Bass.
12. Honeysuckle.
13. Judas.
14. Peach.
15. Fir.
16. Bon Chretien.
17. Broom.
18. Cypress.
19. Nightshade.

20. Breadfruit.
21. Orange (O-range).
22. Olive (O-live).
23. Hound.
24. Lime.
25. Linden.
26. Box.
27. Dogwood.
28. Aspen.
29. Rose.
30. Sloe.
31. Plane.
32. Tulip.
33. Spruce.
34. Tiller-tree or elm (helm).
35. Sycamore.
36. Poplar.
37. Southernwood.
38. Ivy.
39. Scrub oak.
40. Burning bush.
41. Hazel.
42. Lilac.
43. Elder.
44. Cork.
45. Smoke tree, or
maid of the mist.
46. Bonset.
47. Birch.
48. Damson.
49. Slippery elm.
50. Medlar.
51. Willo'!
52. Mango.
53. Sandal.
54. Holly.
55. Clove.
56. Coffee (coffee).
57. Palm.
58. Aspen (as pen).
59. Arbor Vitæ (tree of life).
60. Tallow, snowball.
61. The ashes.
62. Laurel.
63. Locust.
64. Silver.
65. Woodbine.
66. Mace.
67. Vine.

293. Herschell (her shell).

294. It is in a good frame *of mind*.

295. 'Twas the fir ma' meant.

296. They are dissolved in light.

297. Newman Goodman went to the tailor to have his coat mended.

298. Too (2) great ease before marriage, too little ease after it.

299. A jail bird.

300 I X — S I X.

301. He is an imp over a shed. (Impoverished.)

302. They leave them out.

303. I—O—A
Insert W, it makes Iowa.
" T, " Iota.

304. Are—A-re-a.

305. Leg-horn.

306. Because it can't climb a tree.

307. Mr. Dashwood, being at the point of death, sent for his friends and relatives. They sent for Dr Childs who inclosed a few lines to Dr. Barnes and imp-lo-red his assistance. But before he arrived, the invalid died, and the undertaker was sent for.

308. Beat a base drum, or grind a hand-organ.

309. Get up a brawl, or an alarm of fire.

310. (Christmas tree.)

311. Dry-den.

312. A Cole-ridge.

313. Long-fellow.

314. A Dry-den.

315. Their king was A-gag

316. The adder.

317. A-hi-tub.

318. The last two (money).

319. The stoop.

320. When it is a-jar.

321. They are without doors

322. A-gate.

323. Read down and up,
And you will see
How I love you,
If you love me.

324. It is *sold*.

325. He is a *little better*.

326. It is *due*

327. It is a *letter* of *blood*

328. The letter A.

329. He gives it up

330. They are the candid 8 (candidate) of their party.

331. Down in the mouth.

332. Descended from A-ram.

333. There are more rakes than beaux there.

334. Under a pear (pair) tree.

335. Under a hop-vine.

336. Because he is a deer.

337. The letter S.

338. First, they were not inclined to *prey*, and afterwards they were *raven*-ous.

339. He *rifles* the deer (dear).

340. One child from two parents makes 3.

Two children from two parents make 4.

341. Cab-in.

342. 2 and 2

343. The ploughshare.

344. When he " gives it up."

345. A reel.

346. The shade on the dial.

347. They are the grub that makes the butter fly.

348. It is his heir (air).

349. They are more airy.

350. The boy can see his shadow, The shadow can't see him.

351. It has breathed into it the breath of life.

352. A soap-bubble.

353. A clock.

354. He gets wet.

355. It would make *it a lie.* It would make Italy.

356. He carries his reins (heart) in his hand.

357. He may keep a watch, but he can't tell the time of day.

358. The gong makes a *din*, The cook makes a *dinner.*

359. One-sided, sir. Once I did, sir.

360. Cloak—oak—coal—lock.

361. Wood.

362. 301.

363. In the Eastern wars, when elephants were employed.

364. Hat—hate—hatch.

365. Chair.

366. A step farther.

367. The one close their eyes, The other eye their clothes

368. A-dri-atic.

369. The letter B.

Of ell, it makes bell.
" ill, " bill.
" end " bend.
" in " bin.
" rags " brags.
" old " bold.
" one " bone.

370. He is always on the spot

371. The dog worries him. The groom curries him; The dog bites him, The groom bits him.

372. The letter A.

It changed Job to Joab.
made Ner - near.
" her - hear.
" cot - coat.
" gin - gain.
" cub - Cuba.

373. Give him Merry's Museum.

374. Let him subscribe for Merry's Museum, and always pay in advance.

375. It is always expected with interest.

376. The " lap" is the place where infants repose,
And " tea" is a plant that we use;
To " Parley" 's to treat by word, I suppose,
And " pear" is a fruit we all choose.
Many youth like " to eat," I'm afraid, beyond measure,
And part of the head is the " ear,"
And what is more common than, when we feel pleasure,
Or grief, to give vent to a " tear."
" Peter Parley" 's distinguished I'm sure as a writer,
And welcom'd by all with a smile ;
And surely no book is a greater exciter
Than this, which goes many a mile.

377. It is cheap at any price.

378. Merry's Museum.

379. It instructs and amuses children.

380. The one suffered wantonly ; The other from want only.

381. Her-ring.

382. Because it contains valuable articles, wood-cuts, etc.

ROBERT MERRY'S

SECOND

BOOK OF PUZZLES.

EDITED BY ROBERT MERRY.

NEW YORK:
THOMAS O'KANE, PUBLISHER,
130 NASSAU STREET.

PREFACE.

In presenting to the public this New Book of Puzzles, I must present my thanks for the many kind expressions received in regard to those already published. It has been compiled during my leisure moments of the past season, for the benefit of the numerous readers of Merry's Museum, and contains, in a compact form, many of the Puzzles, Enigmas, Hieroglyphics, etc., which have appeared in the Museum, together with many new ones; and is presented with the hope that it may be the means of interesting the young folks around their own fireside homes, rather than seek amusement elsewhere.

ROBERT MERRY.

ROBERT MERRY'S

SECOND

BOOK OF PUZZLES.

1.

2.

3. My first is (in sound) what my second often does; my whole is a turning-point.

4. My first is found in every country of the globe; my second is what we all should be; my whole is the same as my first.

5. The XLNt FX of a 100150500 ☞—H X500er 104i5lty R 1?ab50.

6. Entire, I am a period of time; behead me, I am an article of food; again behead me, and I am used for food.

7. Entire, I am an emblem of beauty; behead me, and I am a powerful liquid; curtail me, and I am a preposition; replace my head, and I am a useful article.

8.

9. Why was Noah saved without a Pope?

10. What is the only word in the English language that can be written without pen, pencil, chalk, or any other pigment?

11. I am composed of 9 letters. In me may be found: 1, a title; 2, a metal; 3, a weight; 4, a coin; 5, one of the Merry cousins; 6, part of a wheel; 7, neat; 8, an adverb; 9 and 10, two prepositions. My whole is a place in New York State.

12. Entire, I am a country; curtail me, and I am an inhabitant of the same; behead and transpose, and I am to prevent.

13.   My first is seen in pillared halls,
        Where kings and princes dwell;
      'Tis found in every woodland vale,
        In every sunny dell.
      Upon the yellow sandy beach,
        The ocean billows roar,
      My next—you'll find it in the foam,
        Rippling upon the shore.

Within the dark and gloomy cave,
　　Hid from the sun's bright glare,
Precious jewels line the walls,
　　And my third is always there.
My fourth and last is found in France,
　　But never seen in Spain;
It has always been in England's clime,
　　In every monarch's reign.
My whole from Jupiter's court on high,
　　Descends to cheer the earth;
Without his presence there would be
　　Of happiness a dearth.

14. I am composed of 14 letters:
　　My 1, 4, 3, 1, 9, 6 is a handsome kind of cloth.
　　My 2, 5, 11 is a conjunction.
　　My 8, 7, 5, 9 is a number.
　　My 10, 3, 12, 13 is to kill.
　　My whole is a celebrated day.

15. 1 YY 1 OWN $\frac{0}{0}$ it.

16. Entire, I am a sentence; behead me, and I am a fortress; curtailed, I am to strive violently; now transpose, and I am inexperienced.

17. Behead a slipping, and leave the slip.

18.

19. A fox, 90 rods due south of a greyhound, is pursued by the hound at the rate of 5 rods to 4 of the fox, the fox running a due east course. How far will the hound run to overtake the fox?

20. What kind of morals are most easily put on and off?

21.   My first is a female,
          My second the same,
       My whole is much dreaded—
         Pray what is its name?

22. I am composed of four syllables, and am very popular just now; my first and second form a Latin verb; my third is a species of animal; my first, second, and third form a kind of rule; my fourth, reversed, is thin and narrow; and my third and fourth, without my final, is intellectual.

1*

23. Why are unprotected hearth-fires like insolent beg-gars?

24. I am composed of 14 letters.
My 13, 11, 7, 3, 1, 12 is a dream.
My 8, 14, 10, 9 is a net.
My 1, 6, 8, 4, 13, 14, 2, 5 is a balance.
My whole is a celebrated man.

25. Entire, I am a noun; behead and transpose, and I am lean; replace my head, curtail me, and I am necessary to the accomplishment of any great object; curtail me again, transpose, and I am sometimes used as a seat

26.

27. Why are most of the heroes and heroines in novels like the letter O?

28. What poet is like a sly piece of bacon?

29.   I cheer the pilgrim's lonely way,
As toils he on from day to day;
Curtail me, and I then am found
What students do on college ground;
Curtail once more, and by inspection
You'll find I am an interjection.

30. What kind of a diary is productive of mischief?

31. Entire, I am a murmur; curtail me, and I signify to produce; omit my first and last, and I am a disturbance; and without my first two I am a bird.

32. My first speeds proudly through our land;
      My next is what my first doth do;
    My whole is one of that noble band
      Who signed the freedom of our land,
    And struggled bravely through.

33. Transpose a wrong way of treating another's regard nto the most foolish manner of doing it.

34. My second, which, by the way, I hope you have, took my first after using my whole at dinner.

35. Behead an animal, transpose, and find a flower.

36.

37. I am a word of five letters; in my normal condition I have a tendency to heal. Transposed, I still have a tendency to *heel*, and have been known to take to them when opportunity offered. Less one fifth, I bathe; again transposed, I am good to eat. Four fifths transposed, form an article much used as an ornament; the same again transposed, is to preserve. Three fifths, properly arranged, will intoxicate. Three fifths, in right order, make a prayer.

38.

39. When did Job call nicknames?

40. Did Jonah cry when the whale swallowed him?

41. Curtail a ruler; transpose, and leave a fastening.

42. Curtail a coin, and transpose it into a country.

43. When is roast beef most valuable?

44. Fair Bessy promised to bestow
    My first upon her lover,
And much I hope that no dark clouds
    Around the pair may hover.

Sweet Bessy's age is just eighteen,
    Of gold she has my second ;
On bearing off the lovely prize
    How many beaus had reckon'd !

And now my riddle I'll conclude,
    And hope you'll not me quiz,
For what I say is very true—
    My whole fair Bessy is.

45. What is that which every one likes to have, and to get rid of as soon as possible after he gets it?

46. My first is found on a ship; my second is a vowel; my third is a title; my whole is the name of an animal.

47. Entire, I'm a man's name; behead me, and I'm a Turkish coin; behead me again, and I'm too close; again, and I'm a prefix.

48.

49. My second is a useful appendage to my first, and my whole is to abridge.

50. I am composed of 21 letters.
My 4, 9, 12 is a Greek preposition.
My 7, 5, 8, 14 a vessel used in the Scotch sea.
My 17, 13, 21 is entity.
My 18, 19, 3, 10 is a bed formed by birds.
My 1, 11, 15 is to dip.
My 20, 6, 2, 16 is to tarnish.
My whole is want of symmetry.

51. A squirrel, finding nine ears of corn in a box, took from it, daily, three ears; how many days was he in removing the corn from the box?

52. My first is found in an oyster; my second is possessed by the nobility; every house contains my third; my whole no one applies to himself.

53. What word is that, of three letters, which, read backward, indicates the quality of many who participate in it?

54. In my first, relations most generally find
An interest of a peculiar kind;
My second, an adverb of humble degree,
Combined with my first names a beautiful tree.

TOWNS IN NEW YORK.

55. A color and a mineral.

56. An element and a game.

57. Part of a gun and a liquor.

58. An animal.

59. A color and part of a house.

60. A hole and a heap.

SHRUBS, FLOWERS, ETC.

61. A vehicle, and where it takes you.

62. A traitor, and the place where he died.

63. To hurt, a nickname, and an engine of war.

64. Take a (1) life preserver; (2) decapitate it and show a mode of using it; (3) again transpose and show how it has been used; (4) transpose and show what is used with it; (5) transpose and give a Greek letter; (6) transpose the original word and make a famous rock; (7) transpose and make a locomotive power; (8) transpose and make it dull; (9) transpose and it will utter a war-cry to dogs; (10) transpose it now into a girl's name; (11) curtail it and express a concurrence; (12) again curtail, and see what you may call yourself.

65.

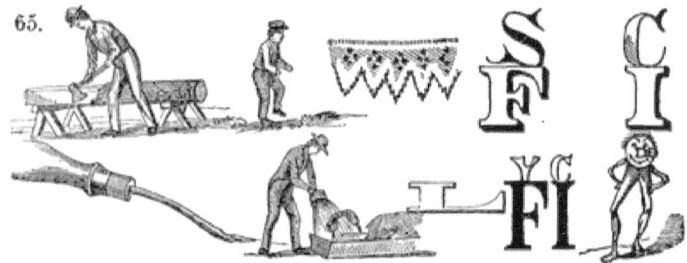

66 'Twas night—a stormy, tempestuous night,
    All wakeful and anxious the crew,
As they watched my first in its wild, mad flight,
    While over the waves it flew.
And now, in the midst of these wild alarms,
    My second is dashed on the shore,
Till Ocean opens her treacherous arms,
    And gathers it home once more.
Let us turn from these dreary scenes away,
    So solemn and filled with gloom,
And in meadows or pleasant gardens stray,
    Where in beauty my whole doth bloom.

67. I am composed of 12 letters:
My 1, 9, 11 is an animal.
My 3, 9, 10, 11 is a grain.
My 4, 5, 7 is part of a barn.
My 12, 2, 6, 8 is a stone.
My whole is a body politic.

68. Behead an article of apparel, and leave one wh
sometimes wears it.

69.

70. Not theory glides not towards rule of action twice
too a Roman coin indefinite article original sinner revolves
ideas use of the needle pronoun boy's nickname theatrical
performance.

71. If you should lose your nose, what kind of one
would you get ?

72. Find a word of six letters, something that many people laugh at; subtract one letter, and leave what many worship.

CHARADE.

73.
A preposition my first;
    My second's a number;
My third a brisk motion
    That drives away slumber;
My whole is a service
    For which dearly we pay;
At least, 'tis charged so
    In hotel bills they say.

DUTCH PUZZLE.

74. Add 2 strokes to I I I I and make nothing.

75. What bird most resembles a peddler?

76.

77. My 1st is in pie, but not in cake.
   My 2d is in hoe, but not in rake.
   My 3d is in house, but not in barn.
   My 4th. is in wool, but not in yarn
   My 5th is in take, but not in give.
   My 6th is in strainer, but not in sieve.
   My 7th is in rye, but not in wheat.
   And my whole is sometimes good to eat

78. Why is a weathercock like ambition?

79. Why is a Turk like a violin belonging to an inn?

80. Why is a used up horse like a bad play?

81. Why is a sick Jew like a diamond ring?

82. Why is a printer like a postman?

83. Entire I am a bird; cut off my tail, and I shall be a surname; now transpose, and I shall be something singular.

84. Why are fowls the most economical things farmers keep?

85. Why is a cricket on the hearth like a soldier in battle?

86.   Entire, I am of bloody mien,
        And spread destruction all around;
      Beheaded—cheerfully I'm seen
        Where pleasure's votaries are found.

87. Why should a brigadier-general, with his troops, be able to cross any river?

88. Join a verb and conjunction, and make a noun.

89. Join a conjunction and a noun, and form an adverb.

90. Join a noun and adjective, and make a verb

91. I am a word of three syllables; my first member is one of the family of fruits; my second component part is an article in very common use, at once a receptacle for the most valuable and the most useless things; my last member is an interjection. Entire, I am a substance employed in writing and drawing.

92.

SCRIPTURAL ENIGMA.

93. Who cowardly a prince did kill?

94. Who built a city on a hill?

95. Whose son profane his life did lose?

96. What Persian queen preserved the Jews?

97. What Jewish king a leper died?

98. Whose wicked mother "Treason" cried?

99.   The initial letters, joined aright,
       A famous Jew will bring to light.

HOW TO MAKE ANAGRAMS.

"Now that's *too* bad!" exclaimed little Bess, striking her pencil down quickly on the slate, which had for five minutes been shaded by her brown curls, as she bent earnestly over it. " I do say it's *too* bad."

" *What* is too bad, Bess ?" asked her oldest sister, Mary, who, apparently occupied with her history, had been stealing occasional glances at the animated face over the slate, and watching with pleasing interest the busy fingers putting down letters, and tripping back and forth among them with her pencil-point. "*What* is too bad, Bess ? I thought something was pleasing you very much."

"Oh! did you? Well, I *was* just ready to have such a good one—these anagrams, you know. I surely thought I had extra axes, and just because of an *r*, it's all spoiled!"

"What were you going to make your extra axes out of?" asked Mary, with a curious smile.

"Now, *don't* make fun of me, please. Artaxerxes was my word."

"Well, I should *think* that would just make it," said Mary, thoughtfully. "Are you *sure* it will not?"

"Don't you see that *r?*" asked Bess, holding up her slate and giving a bayonet thrust to the offending letter.

"Yes; but what has that *r*, all alone by itself, to do with it?"

"Why, it's my *proof*. You see I write down my word, and rub out each letter of it as I use it in picking out my new words, so if none are left, my anagram is complete."

"So you found an extra *r*, instead of an extra axe, in your way? Well, that *is* rather trying; but then there are plenty of more words, and it isn't much work to get them out. You have a capital way. Besides, that wouldn't have been so very good a one. You know 'Aunt Sue' says the word and the sentence should bear some relation to each other. Now, if Artaxerxes had been a famous wood-cutter instead of a Persian king, it might have been too bad."

"But wasn't he a warrior, too and mightn't they be battle-axes?"

Mary admitted the force of this, with a smile, as she went on to say:

"When we see such anagrams as 'astronomers—no more stars,' and 'parishioners—I hire parsons,' there is a certain sense of fitness that produces all the pleasure I can find in an anagram."

"I know they're better; but, then, not half of them *do* mean anything. *I* never could make such ones."

"I should try, if I made them out at all, to have them just right. You must remember it takes some *patience* to *get* them, as well as to *make* them. You want the satisfaction of feeling paid when you're through."

"Patience! I should think it did!" said Bess, laughing and repeating, "Oh, Sam, cut my pen!" in a very comical manner. "If *that* didn't take the patience of Job! And what did it *mean*, after all? I'm sure Webster don't know! I think they ought to be *fair*, at least!"

"So do I," said Mary, laughing at Bessie's earnestness. "Now try the word *homestead*, Bess, and see what you can make of that."

"Why, *is* it one?"

"I'm not quite sure; I was running it over in my *mind* to day; but I had no slate to prove my canceling correct."

"What did you *think* it made?"

"Do-eat-hams."

"Oh, so it will," said Bess, hastily putting down the letters; "and you know they do eat hams at homesteads!" Then Bess began drawing the tip of her forefinger slowly through each letter, repeating slowly, "do e-a-t-h- — *There, now*, that's worse than Artaxerxes! If that *e* was only an *a*!"

Mary looked on the slate a moment, and then said, pleasantly, "But you see it isn't!"

"How easy you do take things, Mary! Now, that would be *so* good, and it comes so near!"

"That's the *best way to take things*, isn't it, Bess?" said Mary, gently lifting Bessie's face by the little fat chin, and looking into her large blue eyes lovingly. Anagrams, you see, may teach us a lesson."

"*Almost* anagrams, you should say," said Bess. "Well, let's try something else. Shall we try 'Aunt Sue?'"

"Yes, put it down."

2

"I can get—let me see—yes, ' use-a-nut ;' but that don't *mean* anything like ' Aunt Sue.'"

"Oh, yes, that will do as well as your ' battle-axes.' You know, she keeps 'nuts' for the 20,000 to crack in her ' *drawer*.'"

"Oh, that's it!—let me send it."

"Very well ; and if I get time, we will try and have two or three more ready by the next number, and every one with a meaning."

When Bess gave Mary her good-night kiss, she said to herself, "I like to get out puzzles ; but I'd rather have Mary's patience than all the anagrams in the world. I wonder if I should try *very hard*, if I ever could be like her !"

ANAGRAMS.

100. Tom can pet lions.
101. Main race.
102. Amy's purple net.
103. Lo ! a slop.
104. O ! hark !
105. I harm the Chat.
106. Hen, I am he.
107. Mid nice rains.
108. I sent one part.
109. Tore a limb.
110. Test Mars.

111. Ira, run, go get it.
112. Cid is a common toad
113. Care on lip.
114. Sal I run.
115. A lion ; capture it
116. Bind sure.
117. Priest tied guitar.
118. Accord I try not.
119. Mend it in a tree.
120. O ! if I can sit so.
121. Is it anger ? no.

122.   Fi rwods locdu fiatsys het rhtea,
       Eht threa gimth nidf slcs earc ;
     Utb oswrd eilk rumsem isbdr padret,
       Dan veale tub typem rai.

     A itleti dsai—nad yrtul isda—
       Nac peeder yoj tarpim,
     Naht shots fo dowrs chwih chear teh dahe
       Tbu venre chout het ahetr.

THE PUZZLE IS, TO GET FROM THE ENTRANCE, **A**, TO THE CENTRE, **B**,
WITHOUT CROSSING ANY OF THE WHITE LINES.

123.

124. Transpose a Persian monarch into a part of the human frame

125. Transpose an article of food into a verb signifying to abate.

126. To what port was Henry VIII. bound when he sought a divorce from his wife?

127. He was ——— who came to ———. Express a truth taught in Scripture by the above, filling the two blanks with the same word taken first forward, and in the second blank backward.

128. Why would it be sure to be better?

129.   My whole, I lightly swim
        The smooth lake's sparkling brim,
        Or down the river skim.
        Transpose me, all around
        The wide world's endless bound,
        In every clime I'm found.

130. My first, you hear its sullen roar
    When wandering by the ocean's shore;
    My second in the gambler's art
    Hath played no mean or paltry part,
    But, fired with sordid thirst to win,
    It often aids him in his sin.
    My whole is something that is found
    Upon the face of all around,   ·
    Yet if you take from me my face,
    I am a title commonplace.

131. If the earth were annihilated, why would it be a pleasant pastime to make it again?

132. My first describes a person, add an adjective and show that person's condition.

133. What is it you must keep after giving it to another?

134. How would you express in one word having met a doctor of medicine?

135. What is that which makes every person sick except the one who swallows it?

136. Why is a person who never lays a wager as bad as a regular gambler?

137. What is the difference between a sun-bonnet and a Sunday bonnet?

138. If I shoot at three pigeons on a tree, and kill one, how many will remain?

139. My first means more than one? my second means a solitary one; my third is highly popular now (with boys more than with their parents.—A. S.), and my whole you are to guess.

140. $A \dfrac{TgEooNdT}{I}, \dfrac{5a50ue500}{but} \& \dfrac{stoo500}{1000is}.$

141. Transpose an animal into a bird.

142. Transpose part of our flag into spirits.

143. In a word of eight letters, the first three and the last three (transposed) name the same animal. The remaining two (transposed), with the last letter, name another animal. What is the word?

144. I am composed of 12 letters:
   My 11, 7, 2, 6, 1 is a place of trade.
   My 9, 12, 3 is a locality where a certain individual passed the night.
   My 5, 4, 10, 8 is a useful animal.
   My whole is a well-known personage.

145. What town in Asia is a fit residence for a wild beast?

146. When does the weather show a good disposition?

147. Behead a crime and leave common sense.

FLOWERS.

148. A raised floor and a letter of the alphabet.

149. An article made by farmers, and an article made by mechanics.

150. An animal, and what he possesses, unless he has been very unfortunate.

151.

152. My second will be better as my first, if careful and energetic as my whole.

153. Why is a drummer the greatest person of the times?

154. When is a sewing-machine a very great comfort?

155. My first is a preposition; my second an animal; my third, in Saxon, means a meadow; my whole we all should be.

156. Three men—A, B, and C—traveling with their wives, come to a river which they must cross. The only boat they can have will carry but two persons at once. How can they all get to the opposite side, no lady being left without her husband in company with the other gentlemen?

157. Straight as an arrow, swift as the lightning, and bright as a sunbeam, I take my flight to the uttermost parts of the earth.

158. My first is a color; my second an agreeable exercise; my third an article of clothing; and my whole a celebrated character.

159. What two female names express a chemist?

2*

160. I'm pretty, I'm useful in various ways,
But if often you kiss me, 'twill shorten your days;
I part with one letter, and then I appear
What young men are fond of all days in the year;
I part with two letters, and then without doubt,
I'm just what you are if you can't find me out.

(Fill the blanks in each with the same word, differently accented.)

161. The—to Fingal's cave would—a stranger.

162. Men sometimes—travelers faiuting in a—

163. To select—often—a writer to annoyance.

164. As an excuse for illiberality, persons sometimes-to the—

165.

COMETS, CONSTELLATIONS, AND FIXED STARS ENIGMATICALLY EXPRESSED.

166. Obstinacy and deceit.

167. A nickname, an epistle, and a laborer.

168. Swifter, a forest, and an affix.

169. A precious stone.

170. Past tense of a regular verb, and a security.

171. A prophetess and a color.

172. Find five letters capable of being transposed into five different words: two nouns, two adjectives, and a verb.

173. Three circles have their centers upon the same right line. The first has twice the area of the second, and is externally tangent to it. The third, of which the diameter is one foot, circumscribes the first and second. Required the radius of the greatest circle which can be inscribed within one of the two equal curvilinear triangles thus formed.

174. When does the weather resemble a lawyer?

175. My first, in sound, is a bird's nickname; my second and third are pronouns; my fourth is three-quarters of what fashionable ladies like to do; my whole is an adjective that has been sadly perverted.

176. My first is a verb, my second a nickname or verb, and my whole is to circulate.

177.

178. Why is a passenger by the 12.50 train very likely to be too late?

179.   Nine less ten,
               With fifty twice told,
          Is what many feel
               When they're growing old.

180. What two letters give a word meaning to debate?

181. Behead an animal, transpose, and leave another animal.

182. What does the boy, in his first surprise, say to his *water-wheel?*

183. What is the political character of a water-wheel?

184. In what coin is its financial value estimated?

185. What is the water-wheel paradox?

186. I am a word of four letters: in me may be found, 1 a verb, 2 an animal, 3 a viscid liquid, 4 a science, 5 a conjunction, 6 a preposition.

PLANTS, FLOWERS, ETC.

187. Part of every animal and part of every vegetable.

188. A beast of burden and a poison.

189. A sweet substance and a cluster.

190. A weapon and part of the body.

191. A household article and what often forms part of it.

192.

193. Dear friends, your notice now I crave,
    For I'm a king, a queen, a slave;
    Each human being claims my name,
    And rightly, too, so where's the blame?
    Although I'm never more than one,
    Just cross me once, you'll find I'm *some!*
    Whate'er my state of toil or rest,
    I always love myself the best.
    I may be greater, never less,
    So now, young Merrys, please to guess.

194. My first is a kind of tippet, my second a Latin preposition, my third is exact, my fourth is a conjunction, and my whole is what my first was named after.

195. a My first (in sound), second, and whole are birds.
b My first, second, and whole are plants.

196. Both my first and second (in sound) are found in the scale. Entire, I am a term of praise.

197. Transpose a coin into some bonds of union.

198. Transpose a bird into an animal.

199. Transpose another animal into a bird.

200. Transpose what we often see on a creek into what we often see (on warm summer days) in a creek.

201. Transpose part of our flag into spirits.

202. Transpose an animal into a vegetable.

203. Transpose the inhabitants of a country into a covered vehicle.

204. Transpose a part of day into a stick.

205.

206. My second is the same as my first, and my whole is a shrub.

207. My first is a bird; my second an insect; my whole is "daddy-long-legs."

208. I am a beautiful tree; curtail and transpose me into another tree; transpose the latter into a useful article; replace the last letter, behead and transpose, and you have a boundary line. Curtail the entire word twice, and you have a picture; take the second and third letters away from the entire word, transpose the remainder, and you have another tree.

209. Behead a hod, and leave a kind of cloth.

210. Entire, I am something funny; beheaded, an entrance; beheaded again, I am a fragment.

211. E10100010001000UN1100ATXN.

212. Deep in the wood of spreading oaks,
   Beneath the tangled boughs,
Where Nature dwells untouched by man,
   My first in luxury grows.
My next in gorgeous robes arrayed,
   Is queen of all her kind,
Where Nature's touch is most displayed
   In beauty undefined :
My whole a lovely garden treasure,
   Emblem of love, of joy, and pleasure.

213. Why is the hottest country the best?

With the letters of the words in italics form the original words to fill the blanks:

214. *I met a gunner* —— his game.

215. *Rob, I came not* to apply the -

216. He was so —— that he did me an *evil turn*.

217. *I mob seven cats* owing to my ——.

218. A —— has often to *mind his map*.

219. My first is a body of water, my second a relative, my whole a time.

220. Which are the most entertaining of bats?

221.

222. Change my head several times, and make (1) a color, (2) a regard, (3) a nickname, (4) to harden, (5) to excite, (6) a mate, (7) an implement, (8) a fish, (9) to form in mass, (10) a part of a coil, (11) to catch.

223. I am composed of 8 letters:
My 7, 4, 6 is a tumor.
My 5, 3, 1, 8 is a fluid.
My 2, 6 is a pronoun.   [man.
My whole is sometimes worn by a lady or gentle-

SIGNS OF THE ZODIAC ILLUSTRATED SO AS TO BE EASILY LEARNED.

Aries the Ram, is a man
ramming down
a gun.

Taurus the Bull, is a fat
John Bull, reading
a paper.

Gemini the Twins, are the
famous Siamese
twins.

Cancer the Crab, is a boy
with a crab biting
his toe.

Leo, is a Pope who lived
in Italy, by that
name.

Virgo the Virgin, is a single
woman feeding a
parrot.

Libra the Scales, is an old
woman weighing
fish.

Scorpio the Scorpion, is a
fierce woman beating
her husband.

Sagittarius the Archer, is
a fat Miss shooting
at a target.

Capricornus the Goat, is a
merry boy mounted
on a goat.

Aquarius the Water-bearer,
is a boatman on a
river.

Pisces the Fish, is two fish
dealers blowing their
horns.

224. The red-lipped morn rose fresh ; and everywhere
    The sunbeams welcome found, save one,
  Which fluttered through the close-barred windows
      where
    The gambling wretches, who the daylight shun,
  With red wine flushed, and eyes bloodshot and
    red,
    Wearied my first.   Again, and yet again,
They the uncertain tide of fortune fed
    With gold ill-gotten, other gold to gain.
Oh, what a ruin here ! of God's most noble
    work,
    Of life's great end, and of the deathless soul !

My second here we see!   Ah, dangers lurk
  Where passions rule—not principles *control !*
In vain my third is raised ; a warning voice !
  Their hearts are hardened, and they will not hear.

Useless to give my whole, or point to joys
   Which but provoke the ribald jest or sneer!
Let us be thankful that the sunlight glad
   Brings to *our hearts* but gladsomeness and praise!
Ne'er be the daylight in *our* haunts forbade!
   Ne'er let *us* fear the noontide's searching gaze!

225. My first is to strive violently; my second is to fasten; my whole is a wizard.

226. Why is it that miserly people have never quarreled?

227. Behead a beautiful product of nature and leave what it often falls into.

228. *a.* A European sea.
   b. A seaport of Russia.
   c. A celebrated mountain.
   d. A town in Tipperary, Ireland.
The initials form an object of interest, and the finals its receptacle.

229. My first is a fluid, my second a solid, my whole a plant.

230. Change my head several times, and make (1) an amateur; (2) to hide; (3) to hang about; (4) a leader; (5) a pirate.

231. Curtail a man's name and leave a girl's name; behead, and transpose, and leave another man's name.

232.

143 When eyes and limbs are wrapt in sleep,
        Within one's comfortable bed,
      My first o'er both will nightly creep,
        With thirsty fangs and noiseless tread.

      My second prowls in every clime,
        Where echoes not the human tread,
      And thick the mountain forests twine
        Their sunless branches overhead.
      And when through groves of oak and birch,
        The backwoods men and maids pursue

For blackberries their jovial search,
  How often have the startled crew
Fled with my whole from sounds they reckoned
  Were like the hoarse voice of my second !

234. My first is a boy's name, my second is a girl's nickname, my whole is a science.

235. Transpose the inhabitants of a country into an animal.

236. O 0. (Good advice.)

237. My whole has two of my first, and is my second.

238. Express with five letters a sentence containing four words and twelve letters.

239. 1CE a horrid X took 2 bt his wife stoo500 a time bearing 1000an de provocation ed but she THEINSTE5IIOLN for he JUcouldRE her came she 500E1000O5OISHE500 ‘ H ¹ I ᵐ M ° with a 100U50uGE50.

240. X A 100.

241. ENIGMATICAL LIST OF ANIMALS.—*a.* A weight. *b.* A whip. *c.* An ore. *d.* A machine used by housekeepers. *e.* A stamp. *f.* To intimidate.

242. The troop arranged for battle
　　　Without my first would fly ;
　　And whether good or bad,
　　　Without it you would die.

　Go seek the earth and ocean,
　　　For smallest things you guess ;
　Yes, bring the atom from the air,
　　　And still my second's less.

　The traitor, when condemn'd to die,
　　　May calm his cares and pray ;
　Yet when the axe sounds "dust to dust,"
　　　My whole he's borne away.

243. Change my head eight different times, and make
(1) a plant, (2) a necessity, (3) a reward, (4) to nourish, (5)
an exploit, (6) to notice, (7) a pipe, (8) a produce.

A RIVER ENIGMATICALLY EXPRESSED.

244. Father plugs an abbreviation.

245. I am composed of letters five,
    The part of speech is adjective,
    From either way I spell the same;
    Pray tell me then what is my name.

246. Entire, I am capital; curtail me, I am still capital; behead and transpose, I am anything but capital.

247. A liquor, a word signifying father; another word for father, a coin, and a liquid measure. The initial and final letters are the same, and spell a title.

248. Take a syllable of two letters from a girl's name and leave a musical instrument.

249.

250. When are politicians particularly sweet?

251. Why is my inkstand like the leaning tower of Pisa?

252. When does a temperance lecturer say a grammar lesson?

    (*Fill the blanks with the same word reversed.*)

253. By a machine many —— can be made from one ——

254. Marks of an —— are often found in ——.

255. My first is an abbreviated name for a young lady; my second comes from the large end of a dog, runs up a tree, and floats on the sea; my whole is required of all persons in time of war, before they leave for a foreign land.

256. When is a fish a rod?

257. I am as black as black can be,
    Yet by a curious fantasy,
    See my tracings, when time has fled,
    You'll find them black, though often red.

258. What is that which strikes itself frequently, and yet does itself no injury?

259. Why are different trees like different dogs?

260. What is the difference between a chemist and an alchemist?

261. Why is a tree like a French dancing-master?

262. Why is a mouse like grass?

263. Why are some kinds of pigeons like drinking-glasses?

264. If a bushel of potatoes comes to $1, what will a horse come to?

265. What is that which burns to keep a secret?

266. Why is a tallow-chandler one of the most sinful and unfortunate of men?

267. Why does a man in paving the streets correct the public morals?

268. Why is an obstinate man like a mastiff?

269. How does the wood-cutter invite the tree to fall?

270. Up!   Stir the rough logs to a ruddier glow!
    And spread forth the gladsome cheer!
For the night hangs dark on the plain below,
    And the swift-winged storm is near!"
      (Full oft my first,
      When loud storms burst,
Shelters some wanderer from their worst!)

"Let the white sail flutter free and wide!
    How our smooth prow cuts the laughing foam!
Faster, yet faster, oh, may we glide!
    For we're going home, boys!—going home!"
      (May the good God's hand
      Keep that gallant band
From my second's wrath, and guide to land!)

"Let the song be heard, the dance, and mirth!
    Glad be each heart, each step be light!
Away with care and the woes of earth!
    Gay be the festal hall to-night!"
     (So the revelers sang,
     And the goblets rang,
While my third kept chime with a glimmering
    clang!)

"To the strife! to the strife!—'tis the trumpet
    calls!
    The foeman comes!   To arms, ye brave!
On, soldiers, on!   He wins, who falls,
    A lasting fame and a patriot's grave!"
      (May God's own might,
      In the hour of fight,
Help those who strive for my whole and the
    right!)

271. Why do trees often change their places?

272 Can a leopard change his spots?

273. White as driven snow are we—
     Black as ink or ebony;
     Red and yellow, gray and blue,
     Golden, pink, and purple, too.
     Glittering like a spangled dress,
     Every color we possess;
     Few and many, large and small,
     Sometimes not beheld at all.
     Thick and thin, and high and low,
     Moving fast and moving slow;
     Fell destruction send we forth,
     East and west, and south and north.
     Fire and flame we fling around
     With a fearful mighty sound;
     Vegetation soon would fade
     Did we but withdraw our aid;
     Dearth and famine would prevail;
     Death would reign o'er hill and dale;
     Never two alike you'll see—
     Puzzled reader, what are we?

274. Add a letter to an animal, and make a building.

275. Transpose a tree into a boy's nickname.

276. Transpose an animal into a famous battle.

277. Transpose a tree into a verb.

278. Transpose an insect into part of a book.

279. Transpose a game of cards into a dress.

280. I am composed of 11 letters:
     My 1, 4, 5, 2, 8, 9 is a Scripture name with which
       we are all familiar.
     My 3, 7, 5, 6 is an article of food.
     My 8, 10, 11 is a nickname.
     My whole is a Scripture name.

281. Why is a man in snow shoes like a man bare-footed?

282. How is it that a man with long legs can not travel faster than one with short legs?

283. I'm worn by many a lady fair,
  In ironing I need much care;
  Behead, and I'm a purling stream,
  Where many a poet loves to dream!
  Behead again, oh! mortal frail,
  And I will cause thy cheek to pale.

CHARADE.

284.   If you a journey ever take,
            No matter when or where,
        My first you'll always have to pay,
            Before you can get there.
        My second you will seldom see,
            If London through you go;
        But still 'tis what I hope you are;
            Few better things I know.
        I say my whole till next we meet,
            When well-known names I hope to greet.

285. I am composed of 9 letters :
        My 1, 2, 3, 4, 5 has done more damage than my
            6, 7, 8, 9.
        My whole is, at present, deplorable.

286.

To remove the shears from the ring—the end of the
string being firmly fastened to a nail in the wall, or some
other object, which can not be put through the handles
of the shears.   (Easily performed, when you know how.)

287. Entire, I am an insect; behead, and I am a rep-
tile; curtail, and I am a conjunction; curtail again, and
I am an article.

288. In northern regions cold and wild,
　　My first you see, a mountain child,
　　In grandeur rise from its bed of snow,
　　And smile on the iron-bound coast below.
　　My second is loved by the school-boy bright,
　　With his rosy cheek and eye of light,
　　And to gain it oft he will truant play,
　　And leave master and lessons far away.
　　In sunny lands, where the fire-flies glow,
　　And fragrant breezes softly blow,
　　My whole you may find so fresh and fair,
　　And who would not wish in that treat to share?

289. Express with four letters a sentence containing four words and fourteen letters.

290. Transpose a dependent into a large party

3*

291.   I'm found in every mountain,
          In every running vale,
      Though never in the breezes found,
          I'm found in every gale.

      You'll find me in the dark,
          But never in the light;
      You'll always find me in the day,
          But never in the night.

      About your form, dear little one,
          You'll vainly look for me,
      And yet in head, and hand, and arm
          I'm always sure to be.

      I'm not in nose, or eye, or lips,
          Yet I'm in every feature,
      In boys and girls I'm never found,
          Yet I'm in every creature.

      I'm found in MERRY's MAGAZINE—
          In Uncle Merry's face;
      And everywhere Aunt Sue appears,
          I claim an honest place.

292. Behead a noun and leave a piece of furniture;
behead again and transpose, and you will find a character
spoken of in the Bible; curtail me and leave the nickname of a distinguished person.

293. Transpose some animals into part of an implement.

294. Transpose something bright into bulky.

295. Transpose a measure into a carriage.

296. Transpose a prop into a source of amusement.

297. Transpose a sudden roll into a clown.

298.   Transpose what a bear might give a cat into what the cat would consider it.

CHARADE.

299.   My first gave us early support;
              My next a virtuous lass;
          To the fields, if at eve you resort,
              My whole you will probably pass.

300.   Entire, I belong to the United States; remove one eye, and I belong to a horse; curtail me, and I belong to the human race; curtail again, and I am the child's best friend; curtail again, and I am best known to the printer. curtail again, and I become invisible.

ENIGMA.

301. Though for years I had lived, I was unknown to fame,
    Till I rescued a slave, and I gave him my name.
    Though then Abolitionist—still I enthrall,
    And unless I imprison—of no use at all.
    'Tis strange I should be both a boon and a blow,
    But when you discern me, this fact you will know.
    Doctors' stuff I convey and small matters unfold,
    Yet rare gems I preserve and great nuggets of gold.
    In form I am round or three-cornered or square,
    And at once I am known as both common and rare.
    If you wish to be safe when you look at a show,
    You must pay for, and take me, and sit in a row.
    Clothed in crimson, and purple, and black I am
       seen,
    Yet in gardens in winter I'm constantly green.
    I am valued and dear, though 'tis equally clear,
    I am scorned and am hated when placed on the *ear.*
    Both of light goods and heavy I carry the trade,
    Yet in gold I'm oft clothed and in jewels arrayed.
    If bad passion disturb, or should ill-will excite,
    I become the forerunner of many a fight.
    Yet stranger than all these remarkable things,
    I'm a gift oft bestowed by princes and kings.

N.B.—As I find it impossible to display all my qualities and peculiarities in verse, I will endeavor to describe myself more minutely in plain prose. I am either animal, vegetable, or mineral, and though sometimes no bigger than a bright copper penny or a silver sixpence, yet I am at times as large as a room—indeed, I *am* a room, and can contain several people ; and then, too, I am made narrow, and can only contain one horse ! In summer and winter I flourish as a vegetable, and am often cut, but never served at table. I am most valued at the end of the year, when I am often given and often taken. Though unlearned, I have given name to a science—a very *striking* quality you will acknowledge, when you know me. If you discover me, you deserve me as a *reward.* If you are dull of comprehension, you deserve me as a *punishment !* May you have your deserts !

302. My first you are when over the ground
    You lightly trip to the river's bank,
  Where my second may always be found ;
    Beware my whole, 'tis cold and dank.
  And fatal, too, to many a one
    Who will not its danger carefully shun.

303. I am composed of 13 letters :
    My 9, 10, 7, 1 was a good man.
    My 4, 5, 13, 2, 8 is an unhappy wretch.
    My 11, 12, 3, 6 is an adjective.
    My whole is an extraordinary tale.

CHARADE.

304.   My first in cities is well know
      And by me many live,
   Obtain their freedom in the town,
      And then a vote can give;
    Iy second we can never see,
   Whether on the land or sea;
   My whole the sailor often braves,
   When he plows the briny waves.

305.   Why may muslin and flour be considered safe articles in market?

306.   Of what trade are we when we walk in the snow?

307.   Take away the bees from something we frequently eat, and make it read and speak.

308.   An animal before a mountain, with the right kind of article, makes a tree.

09.   Transpose some animals into a salutation.

310   Why strains my first his wearied sight,
      Across the silent main,
   And loiters on the lonely beacn?
      He looks, alas! in vain.

   For the chilly hand of Death has passed
      My second's stately side,

And its gallant crew are sunk beneath
The ocean's briny tide.

Though time may pass with silent step,
And years go quickly by,
Yet My whole shall feed the vital flame
And its power shall never die.

311. Entire, I am a companion; beheaded, a verb; re-place my head, curtail me, and I am found in nearly every house; curtail again, I am a nickname; reversed, a verb.

312. My first is "for;" my second and fourth are pro-nouns; my third is an article; my whole is a god.

313. I am composed of 15 letters:
 My 9, 7, 8 is what wicked children often do.
 My 14, 7, 3, 8 affords amusement to boys.
 My 7, 13 is a preposition.
 My 11, 2, 3, 4 is often pleasant in summer.
 My 5, 1, 6, 12 is a girl's name.
 My 15, 12, 10 is often taken from trees.
 My whole is the name of one of our generals.

ENIGMA.

314. I am not found on any ground,
  But always in the air;
 Though charged each cloud with thunder loud,
  You can not find me there.
 Now, if from France you choose to dance
  Your way just into Spain,
 I there am seen, and near the queen,
  In hail, in mist, and rain.

FRUITS, FLOWERS, AND PLANTS.

315. A boy's nickname and a fruit.

316. A bird and a branch.

317. Add what we all love to what we all have.

318. The nicknames of two popular persons.

319. To deplore.

320. Curtail one of the fair sex, and leave one of the unfair sex.

321.   My first, in distant lands
       Full many a temple stands,
       Once builded by his hands;
       The marble from the mine,
       His hand hath caused to shine
       In beauty half divine;
       My next in tropic lands
       Grows where the roving bands
       Roam o'er the desert sands;

My whole went forth—the world,
From chaos rudely hurled,
Along its orbit whirled.

322. Take a letter from a piece of kitchen furniture, and make something furious.

323. Divide a sensibility, and leave a reward and a fish.

324. Divide a measure, and leave something much worn and to desire.

325. Divide something enormous, and leave a plant and to rave.

326. Curtail an unenviable state of mind to be in, and leave a path.

27. Why is a hog just purchased like 120 pounds of steel?

NAMES OF PLACES.

28. The name of a race of men, a vowel, and a Greek word signifying a city,

829. A state of equality and a verb.

330. A letter on a title.

331. Behead part of a vesse., and leave a fish; curtail, and leave tranquility.

332. My first is a domestic animal.
My second is a very useful article.
My third in sound is a Hebrew measure of liquids.
My whole is a list of names or things.

333. Resolve what made Jackson a President into a household article.

334. My first is a nickname; my second, in sound, asks a question; my third is an article; my fourth is an adverb, and my whole is a flower.

335. My first is a verb; my second is seen in a hat; my third is often used for a signal; my fourth is the same as my second, and my whole is the given name of the writer.

336. I am composed of 10 letters :
My 7, 5, 10 is a medicine.
My 6, 9, 1 is an adverb.
My 4, 2, 8, 3 may always be seen on Broadway.
My whole is a city.

337. Transpose a tree into a hollow vessel.

338. D written off for air, hinge learn a channel.

339. XA100T.

Explain the sentences in italics in the following puzzle:

340. I knew a man, not many years gone by,
    Who had a *block of timber* in each eye,
    Without impairing, in the least, his sight,
    Or filling those who saw him with affright.
    And what was more amazing, free to roam,
    Fur-covered thousands made his head their home;
    Two heavy buildings also rested there,
    By them unnoticed, and no less his care.
    A curse upon his meals he often had,
    And saw with joy it made another glad.
    Strangest of all, for every house he let,
    A *half a score of insects* did beset.
    At length he did become *a seasoned dish,*
    To grace a throne, which suited well his wish;
    And all this while *an arrow, mind,* was in him,
    Which to the things he loved did firmly pin him

341. My first's a maiden's Scripture name,
    My second's less than me,
    My whole—ah! so unmerciful
    I hope I ne'er shall be.

342. Change my head several times, and make (1) the cause for some things, (2) to debate, (3) a foundation, (4) that which often covers it, (5 and 6) two different noises, and (7) part of the soil of America.

343. My first is half of what you do
    When you are wildly dreaming;
My second our two horses drew
    One day when Jack was teaming.
My whole the wolves eat when they can,
    'Tis said they love me dearly;
And when I'm stripped to cover man,
    I run about quite barely.

344. What beverage will surely change our pain?

ANAGRAMS.

Fill the blanks with the words in italics, transposed.

345. *Pray, Simon,* that I may be cured of ——.

346. A certain —— used *green soap.*

347. *Cleon paints not* in ——.

348. *Dire loss* is often sustained by ——.

349. —— can *stand carbon* pretty well.

350. *Prejudice runs* even through ——.

351. Transpose a taker into a keeper.

352. Curtail a coin and leave a bird.

353. Entire, I am a mixture; transposed, I am false; behead me, I am a tree; replace my head, curtail and reverse me, I am a nickname; take out my third letter and reverse me, I am part of the body; replace the third letter, behead and transpose, I am a verb.

354. Why is a very large man always sober?

355. Transpose an army into what they use.

356. What flowers are always under a person's nose?

357. Entire I am a dog; behead and transpose, and I am used in almost every house.

358. A planet and a plant.

359. Two girls' names.

360. A certain man's instrument of torture.

361. If you pull a rabbit's ears, what will he say?

362. How does it appear that rabbit's ears are just long enough.

363. Why is a rabbit like a tailor?

364. Why is a rabbit not required to take the temperance pledge?

A LATIN INJUNCTION.

365. Me! men? Tom or I?

366. I am composed of 12 letters:
  My 3, 6, 11, 2 is a *puss-animalous* noise.
  My 8, 1, 9, 5 can make one very comfortable at
    some seasons of the year.
  My 4, 10, 12, 7 is a pronoun.
  My whole is the name of a humorous writer.

367. I am composed of 19 letters:
  My 6, 7, 5 is an animal.
  My 8, 19, 2 is a boy's nickname.
  My 13, 14, 5 is an eatable.
  My 18, 1, 4, 9 is government.
  My 15, 17, 11, 12 are very painful.
  My 16, 10, 1, 3, 17, 4, 9, 2, 11 is ferocious.
  My whole is what we all wish for.

368. I am composed of 14 letters:
  My 1, 5, 7, 14 is a companion.
  My 4, 8 is an interjection.
  My 10, 11, 13, 12, 2, 11, 3 is a scoundrel.
  My 6, 11, 9 is in very common use in the kitchen.
  My whole is a village on the Hudson.

369. My first is an article of clothing; my first and
second combined form a trade; my third is a conjunction;
my whole is the name of a cape.

370. What species of cat has more than one tail?

371. What species of cat is most to be avoided?

372. What kind of cat is most valued in Sunday-school?

373. Which of the cats does a young man show the most affection for?

374. With a hairy animal and an instrument for the hair, construct a burial-place.

375. I am composed of 19 letters: my 3, 7, 5—13, 8, 18, 12—15, 14, 10, 2—17, 11, 19, 5—1, 7, 17, 16, 7, 2—6, 2, 7, 18—4, 15, 11, 9, 18—and 4, 7, 8, 17, 18, 13 are birds; my whole is the name of a bird.

4

376. Entire, I am useful to the student; deprived of my first letter, I am behind time; transposed, a bird in the West; deprived of my first two letters, I am what you all have done; transposed, what you all do; again transposed, a beverage; my whole, deprived of the first three letters, is a Latin pronoun in the accusative case. This last reversed is a Latin conjunction. My whole, deprived of the first four letters, is a Latin preposition; my whole transposed is a crime; again transposed, I am very little; without my last letter, I am used in building houses; transposed, I am used in cooking; again transposed, I am used by shoemakers.

As an enigma, I am composed of five letters:

My 1, 5, 3 is a body of water.
My 3, 2, 5 is a liquor.
My 5, 3, 1, 4 is a point of the compass.
My 1, 5, 3, 4 is a place to rest.
My 3, 4 is a preposition.
My 1, 3, 2, 5 occurs every day.

377. What stream of water contains, (1) a chart, (2) an animal, (3) a toy, (4) two kitchen utensils, (5) three nicknames, (6) an article of clothing, (7) two articles of furniture, (8) a river, (9) a bird, (10) a ditch, (11) a preposition, (12) to strike, (13) quick, (14) a resting-place for troops.

378. How near does a boy straddling a rail come to the President of the United States?

379. When is an Indian like a railroad engine?

380. When are children in danger of forming bad habits?

381. Why is a boy crying to be helped over a rail fence like a lawyer?

382.   I am in the men, but not in the boys.
I am in the playthings, but not in the toys.
I am in the north, but not in the south.
I am in the nose, but not in the mouth.
I am in the minister, but not in his hat.
I am in the kitten, but not in the cat.
I am in the barn, but not in the floor.
I am in the window, but not in the door,
I am in the county, but not in the state.
I am in the pencil, but not in the slate.

383. How far is the President of the United States from the first man that ever died?

384. If a tough beef-steak could speak, what poet's name would it pronounce?

385. Why is a side-saddle like a four-quart measure?

386. What is that without which a wagon can not be made, and can not go, and yet is of no use to it?

387. What does a frigate weigh when ready for sea?

388. Why do pioneers march at the head of the regiment?

389. Why is "i" the happiest of the vowels?

390. Supposing two ships of war, the San Jacinto and Ironsides, to be 2,417 yards apart, at an unknown distance from a fort having a base of $666\frac{2}{3}$ yards. The angle from the San Jacinto to the nearest corner of the fort is $71\frac{1}{2}°$, to the center of the fort $62\frac{1}{2}°$; the angle from the Ironsides to the nearest corner of the fort is $56\frac{1}{2}°$, to the center of the fort $49\frac{1}{4}°$. Required the distance from each ship to the corner and center of the fort—also the distance from a point equidistant between the ships and the center of the fort.

391. With what three letters can you express a sentence comprising ten letters?

392. My first, though originally an animal, now-a-days often goes by steam; though commonly used for eating, is now much used to punch holes with; though hitherto considered rather sheepish than otherwise, in these times goes to war. My second lies before you; waits to do your bidding; is both black and white at the same time; can draw tears or provoke laughter; carry messages and

convey instruction. Entire, I imply a disturbed state of mind, which has extended itself to the body, leading a looker-on to indulge great expectations that something is going to happen.

CHARADE.

393.   On this green grassy ball of a structure called
         earth,
    I have dwelt unregarded for innumerable years,
And none more attached to the land of their birth,
    More deep in its pleasures, its grief and its fears;
I sport 'mid the waves of the ocean and sea,
    Or rest on the bank of some flowery glade.
Or join the fairies who dance on the lea,
    Or play in the checkers of sunshine and shade,
But still I'm intent in my welfare I trust,
    And not to vain empty frivolity given.
When I come to the end of all time, as I must,
    I'm safe in the hope of dwelling in heaven.

394.   Add a letter to a pronoun, and make a preposition; another, and make a noun; add another at either end, and make a verb; another, and make another noun.

395.   Add a letter to a man, and make a pearl.

396.   Add a letter to a Scripture character, and make a flower.

397. A and B set out from the same place, in the same direction; A travels uniformly 18 miles per day, and, after 9 days, turns and goes as far as B has traveled during those 9 days; he then turns again, and, pursuing his journey, overtakes B 22½ days after the time they first set out. Required the rate at which B uniformly traveled.

398. To a word of consent join the first half of fright,
　　Next subjoin what you never beheld in the night;
　　Now, these rightly connected, we quickly obtain
　　What numbers have seen, but will ne'er see again.

399.　　My first it is a curious thing,
　　　　Of Nature's own produce,
　　　And many who have lost a limb
　　　　Have found it of great use.

　　　By my second's wondrous power
　　　　Ships are made with ease,
　　　To stem against both wind and tide
　　　　Across the boundless seas.

　　　My whole is very often found
　　　　Together with my first,
　　　And comes in very handy
　　　　When you would quench your thirst.

400. Add a letter to a crime, and make meditation.

401. How is it that a hen knows no night?

402. Which class of democrats does a hen show most regard for?

403. Why is a large fresh egg like a virtuous deed?

404. Add a letter to a heart, and make a number.

405. What is flatter than a flat?

406. I802500A.

407. Entire, I am a kind of rock; beheaded, I am considered very healthy; again beheaded, I am a beverage; then transposed, I am a meadow.

4*

ENIGMA.

408. 'Tis found in our troubles, 'tis mixed with our
      pleasures,
'Tis laid up above with our heavenly treasures;
" 'Tis whispered in heaven, and 'tis muttered in
      hell,"
And it findeth a place in each sybilline spell;
In Paradise nestled, 'mid Eden's fair flowers,
It has sported with Eve in rose-perfumed bowers;
'Tis muttered in curses, yet breathed in our
      prayers;
From the path of our duty it tempts us in snares.
Deep, deep in our hearts you will find it en-
      graved;
Though in misery sunk, yet from sin it is saved.
'Tis found in the stream that flows on to the ocean;
Though in bustle forever, 'tis ne'er in commotion.
'Tis wafted afar o'er the land in each breath;
In the grave 'tis decaying—you'll find it in death.
It is floating away on the broad stream of time,
Yet it findeth a place in eternity's clime.
In the legends of nations it holdeth a place;
There's no charm without it to the beautiful face.
In thunder you'll hear it, if closely you listen;
In moonbeam and sunbeam forever 'twill glisten.
In the dew-drop it sparkles; 'tis found in the
      forest;
It whispers in peace when our need is the sorest.

409. My first is a drink; my second is feminine; my
third is the cry of an animal; and my whole is a city in
Scripture.

410. Behead something irritating, and leave something
soothing.

411. My first is not so often doled
      To beggar sad and urchin bold,
      As when the full amount in gold
      Was paid for paper one might hold,
      My second is a rank extolled
      As beings of superior mold,
      With virtues rare and manifold,
      When they by toadies are cajoled—
      A rank not made through ballots polled
      By freemen legally enrolled.
      My whole, a fragrant plant, is sold
      In parcels small to grannies old,
      Who in their early life were told
      . "'Twill check a fever—cure a cold."

412. Take the first syllable (which is sometimes used as an interjection to express contempt) from a warlike instrument, then transpose the remainder, and leave some ends.

413. Entire, I am found in Brooklyn; with my first two letters changed, I am a very strong and pretty kind of crockery-ware; when entire, my first is a kind of mountain; my second is found all over the world.

414. My first is annoying, my second (under certain circumstances), alarming; my whole is something frightful.

415. My first is a nickname; my second, a pronoun; my third, a conjunction; and my whole, a fish.

416. Transpose a ruler into a river.

417. Why is silver currency like Cæsar's army by the Rubicon?

418. What boat is found in every ocean?

419. 10050055N.

420. Behead an animal, transpose, and leave a coin.

The puzzle is, to get from the Entrance to the Center Bower, by following the space between the lines without crossing the lines.

ANSWERS TO PUZZLES.

1. W HAIR over each eye (i) n gander or a bound will p over t and v ice beef hound. (Where overreaching and error abound, will poverty and vice be found.)

2. A little patients over a parent wr on g spree vents great miss under stand in-g-s between men. (A little patience over apparent wrongs, prevents great misunderstandings between men.)

3. Crisis.

4. Mankind.

5. The excellent effects of a mild and (hand less h) tender civility are unquestionable.

6. Trice, rice, ice.

7. Pink, ink, in, pin.

8. Think twice before you speak once.

9. He had no need of a Hierarch (higher ark).

10. "Written."

11. Princeton, Prince, tin, ton, cent, Nip, tire, nice, not, in, to.

12. Araby.

13. Love.

14. Valentine's Day.

15. Wise in one's own conceit.

16. Award, ward, war, raw.

17. Elapse, lapse.

18. A chin well rounded is a charming feature.

19. 250 rods.

20. Bal-morals.

21. Malady.

22. Regimentals.

23. Because they are destitute of-fenders.

24. "A celebrated man."

25. Plane, lean, plan, lap.

26. Fin e words r no t all wais t he m ark s of a k in d heart. (Fine words are not always the marks of a kind heart.)

27. They are always in love.

28. Cunningham.

29. Hope, hop, ho!

30. Incendiary.

31. Scowl, grow, row, owl.

32. Carroll.

33. Trifling, flirting.

34. Napkin.

35. Horse, rose.

36. T hay W hoe ark wick limb maid 2 DO ill S hood beak on T in ULE watch ED. (They who are quickly made to do ill, should be continually watched.)

37. Salve, slave, lave, veal, vase, save, ale, Ave.

38. Curtail in g x pence swill lad in Co me. (Curtailing expenses will add income.)

39. When he said "Bildad."

40. He thought he was *going to blubber*, but he didn't.

41. Pasha, hasp.

42. Rupee, Peru.

43. When it is very rare.

44. Hand-some.

45. A good appetite.

46. Mastodon.

47. Casper, asper, sper, per.

48. When there is a will there is a way.

49. Curtail.

50. Disproportionableness.

51. Nine—he took *his own ears* and *one ear* of *corn* out each day.

52. YOU.

53. War, raw.

54. Willow.

55. Black Rock.

56. Waterloo.

57. Lockport.

58. Buffalo.

59. Whitehall.

60. Pitcairn.

61. Caraway

62. Judas tree.

63. Marjoram.

64. Meat, eat, ate, tea, Eta, Etam, team, tame, at'em, meta, met, me.

65. Hew hop lace S C on F I dents in awl purse on swill short L y C on F I D E in no body. (He who places confidence in all persons will shortly confide in nobody.)

66. Snow-drop.

67. Commonwealth.

68. Brogue, rogue.

69. A people intent on being over-ruled by a king, need not complain if monarchs arrogate their ability to over-rule opinions.

70. Practice flows from principle, for as a man thinks, so he will act.

71. The first that turned up.

72. Monkey, money.

73. At-ten-dance.

74. N I X.

75. A hawk.

76. My son, hear the instruction of thy father.

77. P-o-u-l-t-r-y.

78. Because it is often vain (vane) to aspire (a spire).

79. He is an infidel (inn fiddle).

80. He is not likely to have a good run.

81. He is a Jew ill (Jewel)

82. He distributes letters.

83. Dodo.

84. They are sure to bring him full crops.

85. He faces the fire.

86. Slaughter, laughter.

87. Because there is a bridge in every brigade.

88. Donor.

89. Astray.

90. Impeach.

91. Plumbago.

92. Peace to be sure requires justice.

93. Joab—2 Samuel xviii. 14.

94. Omri—1 Kings xvi. 24.

95. Shelomith—Levit. xxiv. 11.

96. Hadaosoh—Esther viii. 7.

97. Uzziah—2 Chron. xxvi. 21.

98. Ahaziah's mother—2 Chron. xxiii. 13.

99. Joshua.

100. Contemplation.

101. American.

102. Supplementary.

102. Apollos.

104. Korah.

105. Hiram Hatchet.

106. Nehemiah.ˉ·

107. Incendiarism.

108. Presentation.

109. Baltimore.

110. Smartest.

111. Regurgitation.

112. Disaccommodation.

113. Porcelain.

114. Insular.

115. Recapitulation.

116. Burnside.

117. Prestidigitateur.

118. Contradictory.

119. Indeterminate.

120. Ossification.

121. Resignation.

122. If words could satisfy the heart,
    The heart might feel less care;
    But words, like summer birds, depart,
    And leave but empty air.
    A little said, and truly said,
    Can deeper joy impart,
    Than hosts of words which reach the head,
    But never touch the heart

123. Watch over your heart to keep out all vice.

124. Darius, radius.

125. Sausage, assuage.

126. He was bound to Havanna (Have Anna).

127. He was *reviled* who came to *deliver*.

128. It would be reformed.

129. Canoe, ocean.

130. Surface.

131. It would be recreation

132. Miserable.

133. Your word.

134. Met-a-physician.

135. Flattery.

136. He is no better.

137. A day's difference.

138. Only the dead one; the others would fly away.

139. Conundrum.

140. A good intention, but undervalued and misunderstood.

141. Wolf, fowl.

142. Stripes, sprites.

143. Cataract.

144. "Honest Old Abe."

145. Aden.

146. When I'ts mild (it smiled.)

147. Treason, reason.

148. Daisy.

149. Buttercup.

150. Hound-tongue.

151. Mode sty i s one oft he chief or name nt s of youth. (Modesy is one of the chief ornaments of youth.)

152. Husbandman.

153. Because Time beats all men, and a drummer beats time,

154. When it is used to sow lace (solace).

155. Forbearing.

156. (1) Mr. and Mrs. A. cross the river together, Mr. A brings the boat back. (2) Mrs. B. and Mrs. C. cross, Mrs. A. returns. (3) Mr. B. and Mr. C. cross, Mr. and Mrs. B. return. (4) Mr. A. and Mr. B. cross, Mrs. C. returns. (5) Mrs. C. and Mr. B. go over, and Mr. A. returns for his wife.

157. Light.

158. Red-riding-hood.

159. Ann Eliza (analyzer).

160. Glass.

161. Entrance.

162. Desert.

163. Subjects.

164. Object.

165. Piece of mind being secured we maze mile at miss fortunes. (Peace of mind being secured, we may smile at misfortunes.)

166. Wilful lie (Wilforley).

167. Willie H. Coleman.

168. Fleta Forrester.

169. Jasper.

170. Had anchor (H. A. Danker).

171. Sibyl Grey.

172. Slate, tales, least, stale, steal.

173. The required radius, 0 feet 1.922257 inches.

174. When it is *a raining* (arraigning).

175. Political.

176. Issue.

177. Be not too wise nor over nice
For if you be, you little see,
How like an idiot you be.

178. It will be ten to one if he catches it.

179. Ill.

180. B and Y (bandy.)

181. Zebra, bear.

182. What a wheel!

183. Revolutionary.

184. In *mills.*

185. While it can not move without a head of water, it never gets ahead of the water, and yet is always moving.

186. Star, sat, rat, tar, art, as, at.

187. Blood-root.

188. Ox-bane.

189. Candy-tuft.

190. Arrow-head.

191. Bed-straw.

192. Patience and perseverance will perform wonders.

193. I, — crossed makes X etc.

194. Boa-constrictor.

195. a. Rock pigeon. b. Rose mallow.

196. Selah !

197. Stiver, rivets.

198. Kito, tike.

199. Wolf, fowl.

200. Scows, cows.

201. Stripes, sprites.

202. Ape, pea.

203. Danes, sedan.

204. Dawn, wand.

205. All is not gold that glitters.

206. Pawpaw.

207. Crane-fly.

208. Maple.

209. Trug, rug.

210. Sport.

211. Excommunication.

212. Moss-rose.

213. Because it bears the palm.

214. Enumerating.

215. Embrocation.

216. Virulent.

217. Combativeness.

218. Midshipman.

219. Season.

220. Acrobats

221. First be sure you are right, then go ahead.

222. Lake, sake, Jake, bake, wake, make, rake, hake, cake, fake, take.

223. Amethyst.

224. Direction (die-wreck-shun).

225. Warlock.

226. They have always agreed.

227. Flake, lake.

228. Book-Case. Baltic, Odessa, Olympus, Killanaule.

229. Liquorice.

230. Lover, cover, hover, mover, rover.

231. Oliver, Olive, Levi.

232. Time and tide wait for no man.

233. Bug-bear.

234. Philosophy.

235. Turks, sturk.

236. Owe nothing.

237. Arm-chair.

238. R U A TT. (Are you a tease?

239. Once upon a time a horrid, cross, overbearing man undertook to beat his wife upon a very small

provocation indeed ; but she understood and overcame his evil intention, for before he could injure her, she demolished him in a little time with a cudgel

240 Tennessee (10 A C).

241. Ounce, cat, pig, horse, seal, cow.

242 Heah-less.

243. Weed, need, meed, feed, deed, heed, reed, seed.

244. Patapsco.

245. Level.

246. Fund.

247 Mum, Abba, Dad, Anna, Minim—MADAM.

248. Rebecca, rebec.

249. C low shoe r heart against awl vice, butt open the door to wall t root h. (Close your heart against all vice, but open the door to all truth.)

250. When they are candidates (candied dates).

251. Because it is ink-lined (inclined).

252. When he declines a drink.

253. Loops, spool.

254. Animal, lamina.

255. Em-bark.

256. When it is a perch.

257. (Often read) ink.

258. A clock.

259. Each has his own bark.

260 One is an analyzer (Ann Eliza), the other a charlatan (Charlotte Ann).

261. It has many boughs (bows).

262. Because the cat 'ill eat it.

263. They are tumblers.

264. A bushel of corn.

265. Sealing-wax.

266. Because his works are wicked, and all his wicked works come to light.

267. He is a-mending the public ways.

268. Because he is dog-matical.

269. He axes it.

270 Independence. (Inn, deep, pendants.)

271. Because they leave every spring.

272 Yes, when he is tired of one place he can go to another.

273. Clouds.

274. Sable, stable.

275. Elm, Lem.

276. Lama, Alma.

277. Ash, has.

278. Flea, leaf.

279. Brag, garb.

280. Jehoshaphat.

281. Because he has-no shoes on.

282. Long or short, he only gets ahead one foot at a time.

283. Frill, rill, ill.

284. Fare-well.

285. Rebellion.

286.

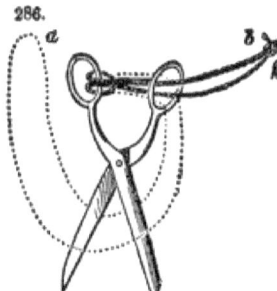

To remove the shears.—Take the loop end of the string; put it through the right handle, and carry the loop around to *a*, as shown by the dotted line here given. Let the loop be carried still further toward *b*, until it has passed entirely around the whole shears, and you can then remove them, as they will slip out through the handles.

287. Wasp.

288. Pine apple.

289. I O U 0 (I owe you nothing).

290. Eleve, levee.

291. The letter A.

292. Stable, table, Able, Abe.

293. Hares, share.

294. Glare, large.

295. Yard, dray.

296. Stake, skate.

297. Lurch, churl.

298. One hug enough.

299. Milk-maid.

300. Maino.

301. Box.

302. Quicksand.

303. Les Miserables.

304. Trade Winds.

305. One may be barred and the other bolted.

306. Printers.

307. Bread and butter — read and utter.

308. Catalpa.

309. Lamas, salam.

310. Friend-ship.

311. Mate, ate, mat, ma, am.

312. Prometheus.

313. Nathaniel P. Banks.

314. The letter I.

315. Bilberry.

316. Larkspur.

317. Heartsease.

318. Sumac.

319. Rue.

320. Lady, lad.

321. Mandate.

322. Range, raga.

323. Feeling.

324. Furlong.

325. Flagrant.

326. Apathy.

327. It is a pig-got.

328. Indianapolis.

329. Paris.

330. London.

331. Keel, eel, E E (ease).

332. Cat-a-logue.

333. Votes, stoves.

334. Polyanthus.

335. Isabella.

336. Washington.

337. Gum, mug.

338. Depend not on fortune, but conduct.

339. Tenacity.

340. Beam, hairs (hares), temples a cur sup on his meals. tenants, eggs salted (exalted), a narrow mind.

341. Ruthless.

342. Root, moot, foot, boot, hoot, toot, soot.

343. Mutton.

344. A little (t) will change pain into paint.

345. Parsimony.

346. Personage.

347. Constantinople.

348. Soldiers.

349. Contrabands.

350. Jurisprudence.

351. Drawer, warder.

352. Crown, crow.

353. March, sham, ash, Sam, has.

354. He is a man of great gravity.

355. Host, shot.

356. Tulips (two lips.)

357. Tyke, key.

358. Sun-flower.

359. Rosemary.

360. Aaron's rod.

361. Nothing.

362. He does not want them made shorter.

363. He is fond of cabbage.

364. He never drinks.

365. Memento mori.

366. Orpheus C. Kerr.

367. Uncle Robert's Picture.

368. Manhattanville.

369. Hatteras.

370. Cat-o-nine-tails.

371. Catastrophe.

372. Catechism.

373. Catechist, (cat he kissed).

374. Cat-a-comb.

375. Blackburnian Warbler.

376. Slate.

377. Potomac.

378. One is a rail-sitter, the other a rail-splitter.

379. When he travels on a trail (T rail).

380. When they linger round the bars.

381. He pleads at the bar.

382. The letter N.

383. A yard and a quarter. *Abe* —Abe-L.

384. Chaucer.

385. It holds a gal on.

386. Noise.

387. It weighs anchor.

388. To axe the way.

389. Because "i" is in the midst of bliss, "e" is in hell, and all the others in purgatory.

390. From San Jacinto to corner of the fort, 1,843 66-100 yards.
From San Jacinto to center of the fort, 1,971 10-100 yards.
From Ironsides to corner of the fort, 2,096 53-100 yards.
From Ironsides to center of the fort, 2,304 75-100 yards.
From point equidistant to center of the fort, 1,763 47-100 yards.

391. R U L. (Are you well?)

392. Rampage.

393. The letter E.

394. I, in, pin, spin or pine, spine.

395. Earl, pearl.

396. Iri, iris.

397. B travels ten miles a day.

398. Yesterday.

399. Corkscrew.

400. Peculation, speculation.

401. Her son never sets.

402. The hard shell.

403. It is a good egg sample.

404. Core, score

405. A flatterer.

406. I ate nothing to-day.

407. Shale, hale, ale.

408. The letter E.

409. Beersheba.

410. Teasing, easing.

411. Penny-royal.

412. Balista, tails.

413. Ridgewood.

414. Bug-bear.

415. Halibut.

416. Bashaw, Wabash.

417. Because the die is cast before they pass it.

418. Canoe (transposed forms "ocean").

419. CLOWN.

420. Deer, ree.

[SEE PAGE 19.]

BOOK OF RHYMES.

PREFACE.

MERRY nephews, merry nieces,
  Merry cousins all,
Merry aunts, with merry faces.
Merry uncles, take your places
  Round the merry hall.

Here's a book of merry jingles,
  Made for merry times;
Merry here with Merry mingles,
Merry groups, and Merrys single,
  "Merry's Book of Rhymes."

Aunt Sue glowing, Fleta flashing,
` Uncle Joe in smiles,
Mattie warbling, Buckeye dashing,
Older crowing, Hatchet slashing,
  Each in his own style.

Merry nephs and nieces, meeting
  Wheresoe'er you may,
Robert Merry sendeth greeting,
Hoping he may have a seat in
  All your merry play.

When in merry circles chatting
  Round the merry hearth,
Merry wit with wit combatting,
Merry's Rhymes will come quite pat in
  To help on the mirth.

THE NEST BUILDERS.

Oh! beautiful, beautiful things!
  How they range at will through the sky!
Dear Mary, if I could have wings,
  Oh! wouldn't I, wouldn't I fly?

I would float far away on the cloud,
   All vailed in the silver mist;
And perhaps I should feel so proud,
   I shouldn't come back to be kissed.

But see, sis, the sweet little creatures
   Have each a straw in his beak;
A lesson of duty to teach us,
   As plainly as birds can speak.

We think they are only playing,
   As they roam to and fro in the sky;
But these busy fellows are saying,
   "'Tis not all for pleasure we fly.

"We're building a snug little nest
   In the crotch of the old elm-tree
We mean it for one of the best,
   And busy enough are we.

" We would not live only for play;
   And when for a song we take leisure,
We would show, in our caroling way,
   How duty is wedded to pleasure."

KINDNESS.

A ROSE was faint, and hung its head,
  One sultry summer's day,
When a Zephyr kindly fann'd its cheek,
  Then sped upon its way.

That Zephyr now, where'er it roams,
  Delicious perfume brings.
So kindness gathers, as it goes,
  A fragrance for its wings.   AUNT SUE.

1*

SNOW-FLAKES.

ARE the snow-flakes pearly flowers
   That in the skies have birth,
And gently fall in gleaming showers
   Upon this barren earth?

Or, are they fleecy locks of wool,
   From sheep that wander by
The silver streams, that, singing, roll
   Through valleys in the sky?

Or, are they downy feathers, cast
   By little birds above,
And hurried earthward by the blast,
   Bright messengers of love?

No, they are pearly blossoms, flung
   From heaven's airy bowers,
To recompense us for the loss
   Of summer's blooming flowers.

MATTIE BELL

SPRING FLOWERS.

WITH what a lavish hand
   God beautifies the earth,
When everywhere, all o'er the land,
   Sweet flowers are peeping forth!

Down by the babbling brook,
   Up in the silent hills,
The glen, the bower, the shady nook,
   Their breath with fragrance fills.

They creep along the hedge,
   They climb the rugged height,
And, leaning o'er the water's edge,
   Blush in their own sweet light.

They seem to breathe and talk;
   They pour into my ear,
Where'er I look, where'er I walk,
   A music soft and clear.

They have no pride of birth,
   No choice of regal bower;
The humblest, lowliest spot on earth

TOP PHILOSOPHY.

CHILDREN must be busy,
  Always something learning;
Toys and trinkets, for their secrets,
  Inside-outward turning.

While the top is spinning,
  Boys are wondering all,
How it stands erect unaided,
  Why it does not fall.

While the top is humming,
  Still the wonder grows,
By what art the little spinner
  Whistles as it goes.

Children learn while playing;
  Children play while learning;
Pastimes, often more than lessons,
  Into knowledge turning.

BY THE LAKE.

MOONLIGHT gleams upon the lake;
Noiselessly the waters break
On the white and pebbly shore,
Then return, to break once more.

Yonder moon, the sky's bright green,
Glitters in its depths serene,
And the stars, above that glow,
Seem another heaven below.

On the white lake shore I stand,
Where the waters meet the land,
Shadows all around me lie,
Shutting out the starry sky—

Shutting out the world around,
In their close and narrow bound,
And the past awhile doth seem,
But a half-forgotten dream.

In the starry night, alone,
Earthly cares and thoughts are gone.
In this silence, deep and still,
Who could harbor thought of ill?

Far from all the care and strife,
All the agony of life,
Who would deem the sun could rise
On earth's thousand miseries?

One by one my thoughts come back
To the old, familiar track,
And I turn me from the shore,
To the busy world once more.

ADELBERT OLDER.

GENTLE WORDS.

KIND words revive the weary soul,
 And cheer its saddest hours,
As dew refreshes drooping leaves,
 And brightens fading flowers.

They fall, like sunshine, round the path
 Of those who weary roam,
And are the "open sesame"
 To every heart and home.

We know the spring will soon appear,
 When round us flies the swallow,
So kind words should be harbingers
 Of gentle deeds which follow.

Upon the brow of want and care
 The joys of life they fling,
And change the soul's dark night to-day,
 Its winter into spring.

Then let your deeds be gentle deeds,
 Your words be words of love;
They are the brightest gems which shine
 In angels' crowns above.   MATTIE BELL

THE FROST.

THE Frost looked forth one still, clear night,
And whispered, "Now I shall be out of sight;
So through the valley and over the height
    In silence I'll take my way.
I will not go on like that blustering train—
The wind and the snow, the hail and the rain,
Who make so much bustle and noise in vain;
    But I'll be as busy as they."

Then he flew to the mountain, and powdered its crest;
He lit on the trees, and their boughs he dress'd
In diamond beads; and over the breast
    Of the quivering lake he spread
A coat of mail, that it need not fear
The downward point of many a spear,
That he hung on its margin, far and near,
    Where a rock could rear its head.

He went to the windows of those who slept,
And over each pane, like a fairy, crept;
Wherever he breathed, wherever he stepp'd,
    By the light of the morn were seen
Most beautiful things; there were flowers and trees;
There were bevies of birds, an... ... ... ees;
There were cities with ter ... ...s; and these
    All pictured in silver sheen.

But he did one thing that was hardly fair—
He peeped in the cupboard, and finding there
That all had forgotten for him to prepare—
    "Now, just to set them a-thinking,
I'll bite this basket of fruit," said he,
"This costly pitcher I'll burst in three;
And the glass of water they've left for me
    Shall 'tchick!' to tell them I'm drinking!"

                      Miss H. F. Gould.

SKATING—WOMAN'S RIGHTS.

WHY may not a woman skate?
  She can walk, and run, and ride—
In dance, or hop, she's always great—
  Prithee why not skate or slide?
Skating is a useful art,
  Full of dignity and grace;
Exercises limb and heart,
  Gives the blood a healthful pace.

Why may not a woman skate?
  Swan-like grace and queenly sway
Mark the vigorous, blooming Kate,
  Sailing down yon glittering way.
Look! what conscious grace and power
  In those broad, out-sweeping strides,
As down the silver-gleaming floor,
  With still increasing speed she glides

Why may not a woman skate?
  Often on the frozen Scheldt,
Buxom Dutch girls, early, late,
  For the prize of speed have dealt.

Sometimes from the inland town
   To the city mart, or fair,
They in merry bands glide down,
   And their precious burdens bear.

Why may not a woman skate?
   To a friend's, long miles away,
Oft they sail, with heart elate,
   To make a call, or pass the day.
Often so do lovers meet,
   Whispering, wooing, billing, cooing,
While upon their iron feet,
   Miles and miles of talk they're doing.

Why may not a woman skate?
   What though ankles she reveal!
Skater's ankles, critics state,
   Are not over-much genteel.
What of that!—a trifling charge!
   There's a right for every wrong—
If the ankle's somewhat large,
   May be 'tis well set and strong.

Why may not a woman skate?
   Six times we have put the question;
No one rising in debate,
   No one offering a suggestion,

Silence gives consent. So, then,
  Pretty girls, and women, too,
No less than rude boys and men,
  May put on the iron shoe.

Try it, girls—ay, try the skate—
  Good for service, seldom tired,
Able to sustain its weight,
  Never weak, nor loosely wired—
The well-tried ankle you will find
  In your need-hour just the one;
Bind your skates on—never mind!—
  You will find it right good fun.

SCHOOL SONNET.

Spell, spell, spell!
A dozen words or more;
To your task and learn it well—
  School days will soon be o'er.

Write, write, write!
A page all bright and clean;
Seize the moments in their flight,
  No lost one fall between.

Learn, learn, learn!
Some useful thing each day·
From early morn till night returns,
  Waste not your time in play.

2

THE LANGUAGE OF FLOWERS.

IT is said that the flowers, as well as the birds,
Have a language peculiar, with phrases and words;
And that oft, in the hush of a warm summer day,
You may hear, if you listen, whatever they say.

I have doubted till lately, and thought it was all
The whim of some dreamer, whom poet they call;
But since the sweet seventh of June, fifty-one,
My doubts have all vanished, like mists in the sun.

As I walked in the garden I saw a sweet rose,
Such as seldom on this side of Paradise grows,
With a deep, deepening blush overspreading its cheek,
Leaning down to a lily, as if it would speak.

Behind a tall orange in bloom, as it spread
Its rich fragrant shadow all over the bed,
Unperceived by the parties, I paused in my walk
And, in truth, overheard an intelligent talk.

First, a low, distant murmur arrested my ear,
Like the memory of tones which in dreaming we hear;
Then, clear and distinct, though subtile as thought,
Their simple, articulate language I caught.

"Thou fairest of gems," said the rose, bending down,
"Too sweet for the earth and too chaste for a crown,
I would thou wert taller, that here, in my place,
The world might appreciate thy sweetness and grace."

"Nay, nay, lovely rose," the fair lily replied,
"It is safer in humble retirement to hide;
Earth's praises I court not; my graces were given
To exhale, in their careless redundance, to heaven. '

As the rest of their talk was of love, and as I
Was acting the part of an eaves-dropping spy,
I will not report it; but this I have told,
As conveying a lesson for young and for old.

THE SONG OF THE EXILE

Blow, blow, ye winds, from the wide blue sea!
  Oh, cool the heat of this fevered brow,
And still this heart with such melody
  As your fluttering wings are wafting now !

Bear on, bear on, from that distant shore,
  The loving tones of a household band
Whose cherished forms I see no more,
  Ye voices dim from my fatherland!

Such sad, sweet thoughts to me ye bring
  Of my own far home with its ivied walls,
Of the vine-wreathed porch, where the zephyr sings
  Through the rustling leaves, and the sunbeam falls—

Of the threshold stone, and the open door,
  Of the kindred forms that gathered there,
At the stilly eve full hearts to pour,
  In a gush of song on the listening air—

Of the noisy flow of the little brook,
  Whose mossy banks our footsteps haunted;
Of winds which half their sweetness took
  From fragrant bowers our hands had planted.

                              FLETA FORRESTER.

THE HARVEST.

TRUSTING in the patient earth
  For the coming need,
Went the hopeful sower forth,
  Bearing precious seed.

Precious seed and full of hope,
  Scattered far and wide,
O'er the plain—along the slope—
  And by the river side.

Softened by the vernal rain,
  Quickened by the sun,
Every little planted grain
  Peep'd forth, one by one.

Nourished by the rain and dew,
  And the genial light,
Blade by blade it upward grew,
  Growing day and night.

Waving in the summer gales,
  Bowing to the blast,
O'er the teeming intervales,
  Ripening to the last.

Duly to the harvest white,
  Goldenly it glows,
As with grateful heart, and **light,**
  Forth the reaper goes.

Brightly as the sickle swings,
  Flashing in the sun,
Merrily the reaper sings,
  While the moments run.

Onward as the strong man goes,
  Fall the golden heads,
Till the grain, in beauteous rows,
  All the field o'erspreads.

Gather, gather now with care,
  Binding up your sheaves,
Save what holy thrift and prayer
  For the gleaner leaves.

Now, upon the groaning wain,
  Pile your treasures high,
Thankful for the gentle rain,
  And the genial sky.

Grateful for the bounteous earth,
  Trusting all to come,
Now with songs of cheerful mirth,
  Bring the harvest home.

Dance and sing in joyous ring,
  Ere the day grows dim ;
Rejoice, rejoice, with heart and voice,
  Shout, shout the Harvest Hymn.

2*

THE SNOW-HOUSE.

"A palace, or a cot—it matters not.

THE SNOW-HOUSE.

See, Charlie, out there, by the elm tree,
  The snow has been eddying round,
And has made, for our winter snow-house,
  A broad and beautiful mound.

Come, Charlie, bring out your shovel,
  And soon we will let them see
How nice, how snug, and how cosy,
  Our winter palace can be.

The door shall be arched and lofty,
  The room within shall be round;
And we'll have a fireplace and chimney,
  And a carpet of straw for the ground.

Then we'll have a magnificent party,
  And all our friends receive,
With chestnuts, popped corn, and candy,
  On Christmas or New Year's eve.

The Merrys all shall be invited,
  Around our board to sit;
They with our house will be delighted,
  And we'll enjoy their wit.

COLD WATER.

COLD water, pure, sparkling, and bright,
    Cold water forever for me;
Cold water *you*, too, must drink to-night,
    Who have come to our apple spree.

For nothing else you will get to drink,
　　Of that most sure you may be;
No *wine*, no *brandy* will we allow
　　At our red-apple spree.

No *cider*, no *rum*, no *lager bier*,
　　Or any such stuff will you see;
But pure cold water, fresh from the pump,
　　We will have at our apple spree.

Drink as much as you will, good friends and true,
　　For nothing it costs, you see,
And in these hard times it is best to have
　　An economical spree.

So a spree we will have, and a jolly one too,
　　And none the worse shall we be
To-morrow, for having joined to-night
　　In a real red-apple spree.　　　　Ruth.

THE GOOD OLD PLOW.

Let them laud the notes that in music float
   Through the bright and glittering hall,
While the amorous whirl of the hair's bright curl
   Round the shoulders of beauty fall;
But dearest to me is the song of the tree,
   And the rich and the blossoming bough—
Oh! these are the sweets which the rustic greets,
   As he follows the good old plow.

All honor be, then, to those gray old men,
   When at last they are bowed with toil;
Their warfare then o'er, they battle no more,
   For they've conquered the stubborn soil;
And the chaplet he wears is his silver hairs,
   And ne'er shall the victor's brow
With a laurel crown in his grave go down,
   Like the sons of the good old plow.

WINTER.

Who does not love the Winter,
  When all on earth below,
The houses, streams, the trees, and rocks,
  Are covered o'er with snow—
When all is fair which once was bare,
  And all is bright and gay,
When down the hillside rush the sleds,
  Nor stop till far away!

And then the noise of all the boys,
  When snow-balls fly around—
The snow-king in the meadow-field,
  With icy jewels crowned—
And sparkling as the purest gold,
  The scepter in his hand,
While icy courtiers, grim and still,
  Await his high command.

And then when evening closes in
  Around the household hearth,
We love to sit while jokes pass round,
  And all is joy and mirth.
And then recount with ready tongues
  The mishaps of the day,
Of plunges in the deep snow-drifts
  When at our joyous play.

And though the Spring may boast its flowers,
  And all its green-clad trees;
Though Summer, with its healthy showers,
  Brings many a cooling breeze;
And though in Autumn with the crops
  Of grain and fruit we're blest,
Yet still I can not help but say,
  I love the Winter best.   S. W.

JUNE.

'Tis a truth that earnest students,
  With books and nature who commune,
Are in thought and feeling quickened
  By the skies and breath of June.

While in boyhood, what could match it?
  Schoolmates call so opportune;
"Come with me and range the forest—
  Recreate, this day of June."

Sister-schoolmates, gathering posies,
  Stop to hear the red-breast's tune,
And laugh at pretty squirrels running
  Up the trees, in leafy June.

After-life, for prizes striving,
  The student toils for lengthened rune—
Spirit (so success) is wafted
  To him by the breath of June.

Month of months—let's sing its praises!
  MUSEUM-readers, join the tune—
The freshest leaves, the brightest flowers,
  All are thine, sweet month of June.

WORK AND PLAY.

WITH mamma for a teacher,
  'Tis easy to learn;
Her eye gives her boy courage,
  As hard pages turn.

She says, "Now, my dear Fred,
  Learn every word right;
If you're patient, the hard spots
  Will vanish from sight.

" When this task is well finished,
  Your *work* will be done;
Then the time comes for playing,
  Says every one.

" Your fleet rock-horse is waiting,
    And baby shall see."
Freddy learned well his lessons,
    And rides full of glee.

Don't tell me of to-morrow,
    There is much to do to-day,
That can never be accomplished,
    If we throw the hours away.
Every moment has its duty—
    Who the future can foretell?
Then why put off till to-morrow,
    What to-day can do as well?

THE BUTTERFLY.

"Don't kill me,"—caterpillar said,
　As Clara raised her heel,
Upon the humble worm to tread,
　As though it could not feel.

"Don't kill me—I will crawl away,
　And hide me from your sight,
And when I come, some other day,
　You'll view me with delight."

The caterpillar went and hid
　　In some dark, quiet place,
Where none could look on what he did,
　　To change his form and face.

And then, one day, as Clara read
　　Within a shady nook,
A butterfly, superbly dressed,
　　Alighted on her book.

His shining wings were dotted o'er
　　With gold, and blue, and green,
And Clara owned she naught before
　　So beautiful had seen.

COLD WATER.

You may boast of your brandy and wine as you please,
  Gin, cider, and all the rest;
Cold water transcends them in all the degrees,
  It is *good*—it is BETTER—'tis BEST.

It is good to warm you when you are cold,
  Good to cool you when you are hot;
It is good for the young—it is good for the old,
  Whatever their outward lot.

It is better than brandy to quicken the blood,
  It is better than gin for the colic;
It is better than wine for the generous mood,
  Than whisky or rum for a frolic.

'Tis the best of all drinks for quenching your thirst,
  'Twill revive you for work or for play;
In sickness or health, 'tis the best and the first—
  Oh! try it—you'll find it will pay.

THE TELEGRAPH—ITS SECRET.

Looking up in musing wonder
At the silent wires above him,
And profoundly meditating,
Suddenly says Mike—that's Michael—
Suddenly says Pat—that's Patrick—
"Can you show me, can you tell me,
How it is that news and letters,
How it is that big newspapers,
Full of news, and fun, and wisdom,
Travel ever back and forward,
Travel with the speed of lightning—
Always going, always coming,
And yet never interfering;
While we, sitting under, watching,
Can not see them, can not hear them,
Can not draw their secret from them;
Can not tell how 'tis they do it,
Can not quite believe they do it,
Though we all the while do know it?"

3

"Should you ask me, Mike"—that's Michael—
"Should you ask," says Pat—that's Patrick—
"How these silent wires above us
Talk, and write, and carry letters—
Carry news, and carry orders,
Though we can not see nor hear them,
Sitting under, watching, listening—
Can not see them, can not hear them,
Can not catch the smallest whisper
Of the messages they carry—
I should answer, I should tell you,
That those little wires are hollow,
With a passage running through them
From the one end to the other;
And they send, not papers through them,
And they send, not written letters;
But they send -these strange magicians—
Through those passages so narrow,
Whispering spirits, living fairies,
Flying ever back and forward,
Message-bearing, hither, thither—
Faithful messengers, that tell not
You, nor me, though watching, listening,
What the messages they carry.'

"Och! indade," says Mike—that's Michael—
"Do you know it, Pat"—that's Patrick—
"Do you know it, Pat, for certain?

Have you seen the whispering spirits?
Have you seen these living fairies?
Have you heard them shooting by us?
Have you heard their fairy whisper?
Tell me, do you know it, surely?
Tell me, is it only blarney?"

Then in anger, Pat—that's Patrick—
Proudly answered, "Mike"—that's Michael—
"Sure you know I'm Pat"—that's Patrick—
"Sure you know I was in College;
Four long years in F——m College—
Hewing wood and bearing water,
Kindling fires, and chores achieving,
For the great and learned scholars
Of the mighty F——m College.
So you needn't, Mike"—that's Michael
"Set me down for a Know-Kothing;
Needn't reckon me a Hindoo;
Needn't doubt that what I tell you
Is as true as if a lawyer
Should have told it to a jury;
Or as if a man in Congress
Or in caucus said and swore it
On his everlasting honor,
On his faith and on his conscience;
This, I trust, will satisfy you."

THE UMBRELLA, AND THE APRIL SHOWER.

KEEP close—we'll crowd the closer,
　The harder it shall pour;
'Tis seldom one umbrella
　Is called to shelter four;
But ours is large and generous,
　And has a heart for more.

Yet faster, and yet faster,
　The pelting sheets arrive,
And our one good umbrella
　Is bound to shelter five,
For we are packed as snugly
　As bees within a hive.

Now let it come in torrents—
　We're snug as snug can be;
What cares our brave umbrella
　For five, or four, or three?
On every side 'tis shedding
　The rain in careless glee.

The clouds are very leaky,
　The bottom must be out,

But, with our good umbrella,
　We have no fear nor doubt,
Though every stick above us
　Rains like a tiny spout.

Heigho! 'tis coming faster,
　The bottles sure have burst;
But hark! the brave umbrella
　Says, " Clouds, do *now* your **worst**,
If you would wet these children,
　You must destroy me first."

They must have thrown wide open
　The windows of the sky;
But, with our good umbrella,
　I think we'll get home dry;
Or, if we do get sprinkled,
　We'll neither fret nor cry.

Step lightly, bonnie sister,
　Keep close, sweet little pet,
With such a brave umbrella,
　We shall not be much wet;
But Prink will have a drenching,
　On that I'll make a bet.

How like a river torrent
　It pours along the street!

Prink cares not for umbrellas,
  To him a bath's a treat,
And our good India-rubbers
  Are umbrellas for our feet.

What's that you say, dear Nellie?
  'Tis dropping on your arm?
Indeed, our kind umbrella
  Didn't mean you any harm;
And soon the good snug parlor
  Will make all dry and warm.

Ha! ha! the wind is rising,
  But we are almost there.
What if our good umbrella
  Should fly away in air!
Run, Prink, and say we're coming,
  And open the gate—do you hear!

THE OSTRICH.

LET the fur-clad Laplander boast
  Of the reindeer's bird-like speed;
Let the Arab, for riding post,
  Bet high on his mettlesome steed;

Let the Briton talk loud of the chase
  With the fox, or the hare, or the stag;
Let the Yankee, stark mad in the race,
  Count miles by the minutes, and brag;

The bird of the desert is ours—
  Competitors all we defy—
A bird of such wonderful powers—
  We scarce know if we ride or we fly.

You have all of the hippogriff heard,
  For mettle and speed a rare thing,
Half-breed betwixt courser and bird,
  Keeping pace with foot and with wing.

The bird of the desert is he,
  The ostrich of beautiful plume,
Skimming earth, as a swallow the sea,
  Or an eagle the lofty blue dome.

He laughs at the speed of the hind,
  For pursuers he feels no concern,
He travels ahead of the wind,
  And leaves the dull lightning astern.

3*

THE PLOWMAN.

TURN up the generous soil—
   'Tis rich in hidden wealth,
And well repays your earnest toil
   With plenty, peace, and health.

Plow with a bold, strong hand—
   Drive deep the glittering share;
No surface-scratching will command
   Earth's treasures rich and rare.

Then, if you'd freely reap,
   With bounteous freedom sow—
And while you wake, and while you sleep,
   The precious grain will grow.

ON A GOOD HOUSE-DOG CALLED "WATCH."

Poor faithful Watch! thy watch of life is o'er,
And mute and senseless near the kitchen door
Thou lay'st, a breathless corpse, where thou stood to
    guard before;
Thy pliant temper, known and praised by all,
Thy prompt obedience to thy master's call;
Whether to climb the hill, or scour the plain,
Or drive encroaching hogs from out the lane;
Thy quick return, on motion of his hand,
To guard the door, or wait a fresh command;
Thy joy to meet at eve, with fawning play,
Domestic faces, absent but a day;
Thy bark, that might the boldest thief affright,
And patient watch through many a dreary night—
All speak thy worth, but none could save thy breath,
For what is merit 'gainst the shafts of Death?
Sleep, then, my dog! thy tour of duty o'er,
Where thief and trav'ler can disturb no more;
Content t' have gained all that thou now canst have—
Thy master's plaudit and a peaceful grave!

GONE—ALL GONE!

By the bubbling fount 'mid the greenwood shades,
In the leafy world of the forest glades,
No more the birds, at the blush of morn,
Trill their sweet notes; they are gone—all gone!

Voices of summer, I've listed long
For the witching strains of your matin song;
Through the woodland dim, o'er the rustling lawn,
I have sought you oft; but you're gone—all gone!

No more do you start in your still retreat
At the thundering tramp of the horses' feet,
Or the wandering note of the bugle horn;
But the woods are mute, for you're gone—all gone!

'Mid the wild wood's haunts, through your lonely nests,
The rude winds play, and the snow-wreath rests
In their yielding curve, while in jeering scorn
The cold blast whistles, "Gone—all gone!"

They say that ye sing 'neath a sunnier arch
Of the azure skies, where the seasons' march
Brings but one endless vernal dawn;
But my heart is sad, for you're gone—all gone!

THE CHRISTMAS TREE.

THE Christmas tree!

The Christmas tree!

O gather around it now;

Its fruits are free

For you and for me,

And they hang from every bough.

Its flowers are bright,
And they grew in a night
For yesterday it was bare
Did ever you see
An evergreen tree
So fruitful and so fair?

Look! here is a rose!
And who would suppose
An orange and a pear
Would grow by the side
Of the garden's pride?
But here, you see, they are.

And, stranger yet,
Here's a bon-bon, set
On the same identical stem,
With two plums, so big
That a neighboring fig
Seems lost in the shadow of them

And here, what's this?
As I live, 'tis a kiss,
And just where a kiss should be;
A tulip full blown,
Hard by it is shown—
Indeed, 'tis a wonderful tree.

Here, bravo! I've found
MERRY's MUSEUM, bound—
This must be the Tree of Knowledge;
Besides which, behold!
All lettered in gold,
A poem fresh out from the college.

Hold! hold! my good sirs,
Here's a nice set of furs—
'Tis a fir-tree, you all must agree;
And here, not *incog.*,
Is a sweet sugar-hog—
Does that make a mahogany-tree?

Oh! who would have guessed?
Here's a nice little chest,
Of course 'tis a chestnut-tree;
Not so fast, cousin Knox,
Here's a beautiful box—
A box-tree it surely must be.

Your proof something lacks,
For here is an ax.
You must own 'tis an axle-tree now;
Hallo! here's a whip,
For your horsemanship—
'Tis a whipple-tree, then, you'll allow.

What now shall be said?
Here are needles and thread—
Let's see—shall we call it tre-mend(o)us?
Oh, pshaw! pray do stop,
I'm ready to drop—
Your puns are absurdly stupendous.

MY MOTHER'S BIRTHPLACE.

IT was just outside of the village,
  In a cool, sequestered nook,
On the right was the murmuring forest,
  On the left was the babbling brook.
Behind, the o'ershadowing mountain
  Reared its gray old head to the sky,
While before it, the widening valley
  Stretched out like a sea to the eye.

'Twas a rare, sweet spot, and a lovely
  As ever this fair world knew;
There spring came earliest always,
  And summer the latest withdrew.
Day reluctantly left it at evening,
  And hastened to greet it at dawn,
And stars, birds, and flowers loved to visit
  THE PLACE WHERE MY MOTHER WAS BORN.

THE SONG OF BOB LINCOLN.

BY UNCLE TIM.

It was a beautiful morning, quite early in May,
The fathers all plowing, the children all play;
The mothers all spinning, as busy as bees,
And the birds quite as busy all round in the trees;
While some were singing songs over and over,
Sometimes in the tree-tops, then down in the clover,
Young Robert was trying his very best notes,
And the strength of his song by the length of his throat.

> Chorus—Envy me, envy me,
> Cordially, cordially,
> Fiddlesticks, fiddlesticks!
> Just act your pleasure, sir.

Sometimes he was singing to Jemmy the farmer,
And then to Miss Alice, and trying to charm her;
Next moment he'd light on the top of a thistle,
And either be singing or trying to whistle:
Miss Alice, Miss Alice! it will give me much pleasure
To sing you a sonnet while I am at leisure.
I will sing you a good one, and very explicit,
And stop when I choose, or whenever you wish it.

> Chorus—Certainly, certainly, etc.

While Jemmy is plowing and learning to whistle,
My wife is at home, in the shade of a thistle,
In a neat little nest, with a wild rose behind it.
You need not look for it, for you never can find it.
The farmer is plowing, and soon will be mowing;
While he's cutting the daisies his corn will be growing.
When the heads on the barley are ripe, and the cherry,
Mary Lincoln and I will be singing so merry.

> CHORUS—Cordially, cordially,
> Envy me, envy me,
> Fiddlesticks, fiddlesticks!
> Just act your pleasure, sir.

When the leaves on the trees and the flowers on the
    clover
Are withered and faded, and Summer is over;
When the grass on the meadows is leveled and gone,
We will sing our last sonnet and leave you alone.
We will fly far away to the rice and the cotton;
But let not our thistle and rose be forgotten.
We are certain to come again early in Spring,
And bring some choice music, which we promise to
    sing.

> CHORUS—Cordially, cordially,
> Envy me, envy me,
> Fiddlesticks, fiddlesticks!
> Just act your pleasure, sir.

A WILL AND A WAY.

A LAPLAND merchant must needs, one day,
    To a distant market go;
But he had no horse, and he had no sleigh,
    To carry him over the snow.

"Yet go I must," said the sturdy man—
    "There is a way for every will—
Each new necessity has its plan,
    For the earnest mind to fulfill."

So he drew, from the ice-bound river, a scow,
    And lined it with furs and moss,
Then harnessed a reindeer to its prow,
    With a rope his horns across.

No track was there—but the traveler knew
 The way over valley and plain;
Like a well-trained steed, the reindeer flew,
 And brought him safe back again.

The fashion he set is in fashion now,
 Among the fur-clad Norse;
They use for a sleigh a flat-bottomed scow,
 And a reindeer for a horse.

Said the resolute man, " They shall serve my turn;
 Whatever we must, we may,
And sooner or later each man will learn,
 That *where there's a will there's a way.*"

BLOWING BUBBLES.

THE boys were blowing bubbles,
  Bright red, and green, and blue,
And every changing color
  That ever mortal knew.
They floated in the window,
  And glided past my chair,
But in a moment perishod,
  And faded in the air.

The boys, with shouts and laughter,
    Blew till quite out of breath,
While high in the leafy maple
    The bubbles gleamed till death.
Too much like earthly pleasure
    Seemed the bubbles, bright and gay ;
They charm a fleeting moment,
    Then vanish, away—away.

Sweet love's ecstatic potion
    Our spirits long to sip,
But Death may dash the nectar
    From the unsullied lip.
And he who quaffs the longest,
    Whose heart divinely glows,
Finds clouds will gather round him,
    For earthly joys must close.

Some grasp at wealth's bright beacon,
    And follow where it leads—
Sometimes to fairest honor,
    Sometimes to foulest deeds
And often proves a bubble,
    A floating thing of air—
Eludes the weary victim,
    And leaves him starving there.

If love's so frail a treasure,
  And wealth may fade away:
If earthly joys are changing,
  And fame lives but a day;
Then where are shining jewels
  That will not break at last,
And leave us, eager viewers,
  All mourning for the past?

High in the holy heavens,
  A pearl of price untold
Shines brighter far than rubies,
  More precious than fine gold.
It can not fade or perish,
  Can never pass away;
It is a hope in Jesus,
  A trust in God alway!   M. A. L.

AFTER SCHOOL.

Just look upon that group of boys,
Brim full of frolic, spunk, and noise,
When, at the word, "The school is done,"
They rush to liberty and fun.

Pell-mell, they run, and jump, and leap,
Tumbling in one promiscuous heap,
Until you wonder by what token
They 'scape with heads and limbs unbroken.

Bold, reckless, cunning, cool, or sly,
What won't they do? what won't they try?
They're up to every kind of scheme,
To test their strength, and let off steam.

'Tis an epitome of life,
Without its shades of care and strife;
Each has his private joke, and cracks it,
Regardless how the other takes it.

And there's the point—boys take rough jokes
More pleasantly than older folks,
Not heeding much what's said or done,
So they can have their fill of fun.

THE NIGHTINGALE.

Sweet bird! that through the shadows
  Of the night, so sad and lone,
Warblest thy notes of gladness,
  With softly thrilling tone.

'Tis when the gloom is deepest,
  And all is hushed in fear,
Save that night-winds are moaning
  Through the stillness dark and drear;

'Tis then thy voice is sweetest,
  And seems wafted from above,
As to the sad and sorrowing
  Come words of hope and love.

Thou'rt heard within the casement,
  Through the weary night of pain;
And thy warble is an earnest
  That the day will come again.

Methinks thou art a spirit-bird,
  Sent from a holier sphere;
Such spirits do not linger
  Amidst the sorrowing here.

LEAP-FROG.

THAT'S right, Benny, go it strong,
Go it high, and go it long,
Swiftly run, and boldly leap,
Froggy Charles is quite a heap.

Charley Frog, now take your jump;
Benny, make yourself a lump;
'Tis a wholesome sport and rare—
Rest and toil an equal share.

Now you're down, and now you're up;
Now you leap, and now you stoop;
Now you rest, and now you run;
Any way, 'tis right good fun.

A WORLD OF LOVE AT HOME

THE earth hath treasures fair and bright.
  Deep buried in her caves,
And ocean hideth many-a gem
  With his blue, curling waves;
Yet not within her bosom dark,
  Or 'neath the dashing foam,
Lives there a treasure equaling
  A world of love at home!

True, sterling happiness and joy
  Are not with gold allied,
Nor can it yield a pleasure like
  A merry fireside.
I envy not the man who dwells
  In stately hall or dome,
If, 'mid his splendor, he hath not
  A world of love at home.

The friends whom time hath proved sincere,
  'Tis they alone can bring
A sure relief to hearts that droop
  'Neath sorrow's heavy wing.
Though care and trouble may be mine,
  As down life's path I roam,
I'll heed them not while still I have
  A world of love at home.

I MUST HASTEN HOME.

I MUST hasten home, said a rosy child,
    Who had gayly roamed for hours ;
I must hasten home to my mother dear—
    She will seek me amid the bowers.
If she chides, I will seal her lips with a kiss,
    And offer her all my flowers.

I must hasten home, said a beggar girl,
    As she carried the pitiful store

Of crumbs and scraps of crusted bread,
     She had gathered from door to door;
I must hasten home to my mother dear—
     She is feeble, and old, and poor!

I must hasten home, said the ball-room belle,
     As day began to dawn;
And the glittering jewels her dark hair decked,
     Shone bright as the dews of morn;
I'll forsake the joys of this changing world,
     Which leave in the heart but a thorn.

I must hasten home, said a dying youth,
     Who had vainly sought for fame—
Who had vowed to win a laurel wreath,
     And immortalize his name;
But, a stranger, he died on a foreign shore-
     All the hopes he had cherished were vain.

I am hastening home, said an aged man,
     As he gazed on the grassy sod,
Where oft, ere age had silvered his hairs,
     His feet had lightly trod;
Farewell! farewell to this lovely earth—
     I am hastening home to God!

THE EVENING PRAYER.

WITH meek and simple faith,
　　A child's confiding love,
The infant cherub kneels to breathe
　　His prayer to God above.
And all the host of heaven is there,
To listen to that infant prayer.

" God, bring dear father home,
　　God, make dear mother well,
God, make me good, and let us come
　　All in Thy house to dwell."
Then, while their watch good angels keep,
" God giveth His beloved sleep."

ACROSTIC.

Roses and tulips, with all their gay train,
O'er garden and landscape cause beauty to reign.
By the brook, or the hillside, or light woody grove,
Enchanted—delighted—on, smiling, we rove;
'Rapt up in fond thoughts of the verdure and bloom,
'Till autumn's cold frost sweeps the whole to the tomb.

My emotions, when life seems thus passing and vain,
Even wisdom and prudence can hardly restrain.
Rude winter now comes, and with sleet, hail, and snow,
Right and left sends his arrows, as shivering we go.
Yet I see there's a chance, even *now*, to be cheery,
Sitting snug by the fire, with old *Robert Merry*.

My cosy old friend, no winter is found
Unfurled in thy pages the whole season round!
Still birds sing their songs in some warm, sunny clime,
Ever speaking in music and talking in rhyme;
Unless you may tell us some odd tale that's true,
Making all of us merry, *Old Merry*, with you!

B.

OUR NEBBY.

Sure I am, I do not know
Why we love our Nebby so;
But I am sure, as sure can be,
Nebby knows why he loves me.
Mattie feeds Neb every day,
And 'tis as good as any play,
Just to see his pranks and freaks,
When to Nebby Mattie speaks.
When I go home from the store,
Nebby meets me at the door,
And says, most eloquently dumb,
"Nebby 's glad that you have come."
Nebby is a little pet;
Nebby don't know how to fret;
But he knows the tenderest part
Of our Mattie's tender heart.

THE NEW SONG.

WHENCE that sweet, inspiring strain,
   Pealing on my ravished ear?
Hark! its thrilling notes again
   From the courts of heaven I hear—
" Hallelujah to the Lamb,
   Who hath bought us with His blood!
Honor, glory to His name,
   We through Him are sons of God."
Angels fain their notes would join
   With that vast, triumphant song;
But *their* harps, though all divine,
   Ne'er can reach that wondrous song.
Learned on earth, and new in heaven,
   Only they its chords can know
Who to God by grace are given,
   Ransomed from the depths of wo.
Angels can not know or tell,
   In their pure, unfallen bliss,
How a soul, redeemed from hell,
   Sings the mystery of grace!
They the chosen, countless throng,
   Ever round the throne above,
In their new and endless song,
   Celebrate redeeming love.

THE CHINAMAN.

THE Chinaman his life consumes,
  On opium regaling—
The Yankee his tobacco fumes
  With equal zest inhaling—
Though trembling nerves and fitful glooms
  Warn them that health is failing.

For almost everything that's done
  Some reason wit supposes,
But for the smoker's faith, not one
  The keenest wit discloses ;
'Tis filthy, vulgar, costly fun,
  Hateful to all good noses.

AN INDIAN DANDY.

WELL, isn't that a funny dress?
You think he must be cruel,
With human bones set round his crown,
And skulls in place of jewels.

Yet in his countenance you see
  Nothing severe or savage,
As if, with cannibal intent,
  Our whole domain he'd ravage.

There's no accounting for our tastes,
  (" *De gustibus*," and so forth ;)
Some dote on very slender waists,
  Some like hooped cisterns go forth.

Sneer not at Indian or Malay,
  Nor get into a passion ;
He does as you do day by day—
  Follows the latest fashion.

White dandies strut in stove-pipe hats,
  White women go bare-headed :
Which is most proper, red or white,
  We leave in doubt deep shaded.

5*

THE SHADOW.

ONE sunny day a child went Maying—
When lo, while 'mid the zephyrs playing,
He saw his shadow at his back !
He turned and fled, but on his track
The seeming goblin came apace,
And step for step gave deadly chase !

Weary at last, with desperate might
The urchin paused and faced the fright,
When lo, the demon, thin and gray,
Faded amid the grass away !

'Tis thus in life—when shadows chase,
If we but meet them face to face,
What seemed a fiend in fear arrayed,
Sinks at our feet a harmless shade.

                                    PETER PARLEY.

CONTENTS.

	PAGE
The Nest Builders	7
Kindness	9
Snow Flakes	11
Spring Flowers	12
Top Philosophy	13
By the Lake	15
Gentle Words	17
The Frost	18
Skating--Woman's Rights	21
School Sonnet	25
The Language of Flowers	27
The Song of the Exile	29
The Harvest	31
The Snow House	35
Cold Water	36
The Good Old Plow	39
Winter	40
June	43
Work and Play	44
The Butterfly	46
Cold Water	48
The Telegraph—its Secret	49
The April Shower	53
The Ostrich	56
The Plowman	57
The House-Dog " Watch'	59

	PAGE
Gone- all Gone	61
The Christmas Tree	62
My Mother's Birthplace	66
The Song of Bob Lincoln	67
A Will and a Way	69
Our Garret	71
Charley and his Boat	74
Blessed is he that Considereth the Poor	75
The Dissatisfied Angler Boy	77
The Destroyer Destroyed	79
The Rose in the Vale	81
Of What is the Alphabet Composed?	88
Geography and Astronomy	83
Going to School	84
The Way to Do It	85
When One Won't Quarrel, Two Can't	85
The Caterpillar	87
The Warning Bell	88
Blowing Bubbles	89
After School	93
The Nightingale	94
Leap Frog	95
A World of Love at Home	96
I must Hasten Home	97
The Evening Prayer	99
Acrostic	100
Our Nebby	101
The New Song	102
The Chinaman	108
The Indian Dandy	104
The Shadow	106